Thirty Seven Guns

Tricia Price

TSL Publications

First published in Great Britain in 2018
By TSL Publications, Rickmansworth

ISBN / 978-1-911070-16-0

Cover photo: https://pixabay.com/en/travel-city-athens-acropolis-
2152792/;
https://commons.wikimedia.org/wiki/File:Lord_Byron_in_Albanian_
dress.jpg

AUTHOR'S NOTE

Few holidays can have had so profound an influence on subsequent events as the Greek tour undertaken in his youth by the sixth Lord Byron.

That influence was so significant that in correlating the two Greek episodes of this notorious life I make no apology for presenting "another Byron book".

PRELUDE

In September of the year 1809, the greater part of the civilized western world lay under the shadow of Napoleon Bonaparte, and a continent reeled at the shock of opposing armies. But while the newly modelled army of parvenu England, recovered from the blood and smoke of Corunna, had retaliated strongly at Talavera, and the Peninsula War was a year old, an aged aristocrat at Europe's further edge was sinking still deeper into the mud of degradation and oppression. The glory that was Greece, a splendid memory, made little impact now upon the course of world history. Her civilization had perished and her people dwindled; her buildings had crumbled and her laws evaporated; and her gods rendered homage to Islam. The poorest English rustic would have thought himself well-to-do compared with many a Levantine peasant: despite its attendant human miseries, the increasing industrial sprawl of England brought prosperity and a fierce patriotism in its wake, while Greece struggled along from day to day scraping a living from the sun-baked soil and accepting foreign rule with resignation and apathy.

One morning in this September of 1809, a brig had set sail from the Gulf of Patras, heading for Previsa. Leaving behind the mountains and the foothills green with groves of oranges and lemons, dotted with the glitter of minarets, she headed out of the bay and across the gulf until, towards sunset, there came into view a range of mountains rising one behind the other as far as the eye could see and, at their feet, a curious double fore-shore. The strange appearance of the beach attracted the attention of a passenger on board the brig – a young man, a little above average height, perhaps a little plump, wrapped in a long boat-cloak. The finely-shaped head, with auburn hair curling above a high brow, the large and well-shaped nose, the full-cut mouth, short upper lip and even white teeth would not have seemed out of place on one of the Olympian deposed, had not the aristocratic nose been a trifle thick and one grey eye larger than the other – discrepancies to mar a divine but to add character to a human countenance.

A footstep sounded behind him. The young man turned and asked the passing Levantine in a soft, clear voice with a hint of a drawl, "What place is that, yonder – with the curious foreshore?"

"That, Mylord*?" The other's voice held a surprised note. "A poor place, unworthy of your honour's attention. They call it Missolonghi."

"Missolonghi? Missolonghi. A strange name, like a sigh. A haunting name. I fear that it will haunt me – *has* haunted me."

The other man looked curiously, wondering if the English Mylord were mad, not liking to speak again.

"It fades into the night – but it will return. Or I shall return. So strange – yet I seem to have known it always."

The brig sailed steadily northward. Soon Ulysses' own island would appear, a dim shadow to port. But still the figure in the cloak stood motionless, his gaze transfixed, mesmerised. And two pairs of eyes watched Missolonghi drawn into the gathering dusk.

---

* Nickname for Byron

PART ONE
THE LAURELS

The Secretary's welcome was effusive, delighted and never-ending. Mr John Cam Hobhouse, forced into unwilling admiration of his fluency, wished fervently that his friend would come and assist him – surely the fellow wasn't such a dandy that his toilet must occupy him this age. The third person in the room, a priest, was mercifully silent – speaking neither French nor English, he must content himself perforce with bowing and beaming whenever the Englishman looked his way.

The Secretary was still speaking. "But it is a matter for the utmost congratulation! To have crossed the perilous seas from your northern island – what bravery! And to have penetrated safely to His Highness's capital despite the brigands – I do trust and hope you were not molested?"

"We met one or two tough characters but no footpads, I assure you. And yesterday a gun was fired close at hand, but that I believe was the work of a shepherd only."

"Tck-tck! They are unlettered oafs, our native shepherds" – Hobhouse smiled involuntarily at the "our" – "and know no better. But you will find no such discourtesy here at Iannina. You may be assured of my personal attention to your slightest desire."

Hobhouse bowed his gratitude – the priest bowed back.

The spate of words flowed on. "Iannina is, of course, most happy – and most honoured – to be your host. His Highness is desolated that he is not at present here to entertain you in person. He has been obliged to leave on an affair of some small moment – *une petite guerre*, you understand, which absorbs his attention. Ibrahim Pasha is proving a little – difficult. Always is it thus!" The Secretary sighed.

Hobhouse was courteously sympathetic. (Heavens, how much

longer must he handle this alone?) "It is not unusual?"

The Secretary shrugged. "What would you? The province is large, and the people do not always understand what is for their good. They are simple folk who need assistance in the management of their affairs. Fortunately for them, there is always the Pasha to show them the way. Ah," – with perfect truth – "there is no one like Ali."

"Indeed his fame has spread far. We shall be sorry to have missed an audience with so renowned a man."

"But you shall not! Everything here has been fully ordered for your comfort, and the Vizier himself begs that you will deign to follow him, that he may receive you as befits your high degree. It is not every day that such noble visitors enter our capital. When you shall have recovered from the effects of this already arduous journey, an escort shall be provided, and all shall be ready as and when you command."

The Secretary paused for breath: the priest bowed: and Hobhouse, to his great relief, was spared the necessity of an immediate answer by the opening of the door. The three men turned as one to meet the newcomer – a young man a little above average height, with a slight tendency to plumpness, glossy chestnut hair curling thickly over his head, and clear grey eyes which sparkled expressively in a strikingly handsome face. He came forward with a slight limp occasioned by a twist in his right foot – hidden from view by the long pantaloons strapped down over his feet. There was a certain hesitancy in his manner, as if, too conscious himself of his infirmity, he would defend himself from curious gaze.

The Secretary was off again. "And this must surely be Mylord. So noble a countenance can belong to no one else." Lord Byron, a little startled by this flattering candour, bowed his recognition. The priest bowed back, happily. "His Highness is indeed honoured by this visit. As I have already informed Mr Hobhouse, the Pasha has left Iannina on a small matter of business, but he hopes to welcome you in the North very soon. And if you will permit, I shall myself accompany you and sustain you on the way." Again Hobhouse's lips twitched involuntarily, but Byron maintained his composure. "As Inspector, it is necessary that I should render account to the Pasha."

"We shall be very glad of your company," Byron assured him. "Company must always be welcome in a strange country."

"Mylord is too gracious. Perhaps you would care to survey this unworthy town while the necessary preparations are made?"

"It would surely be a pity to come so far without exploring. We shall be very happy to see what Iannina has to offer of beauty and interest."

"You would like to visit the Bey, perhaps? He would be most highly honoured to receive you in his grandfather's stead. He is a most charming and courteous young man – you cannot but be delighted with him. And, Mylord, before I shall go – I must insist that all the charges of your provisioning during your stay here shall be laid to the Vizier's purse. It must not be otherwise – it is His Highness's express wish. Now we depart – our visitors must be in need of refreshment, from which we have kept them too long. Please call on me, personally, for anything which you find lacking in the arrangements."

The priest bowed; the Secretary bowed; both gentlemen raised, with some difficulty, the enormous caps which distinguished their rank, taking both hands to the task. A short commotion took place at the door as the two gentlemen shuffled into their outer shoes and bowed each other out with great formality. The scuffle was almost too much for their hosts' gravity; amused and embarrassed, the two young men avoided each others' eyes as they murmured their *adieux*, which were received with courteous dignity. As the sound of their footfalls died away, the bottled-up merriment burst forth, and would not be denied.

"Oh John, John!" cried Byron, clutching at a chairback. "How shall you be sustained?"

"Well enough if the Pasha commands it," answered Hobhouse drily. "Upon my soul, he must be a noble fellow to treat strangers at his gate so royally. I wish all landlords were as generous – they're a thieving set of rascals in my experience."

"Ah, but then your experience is limited," his friend pointed out provocatively, his eyes glinting mischievously. "You should accompany me more often – that brings its own honour, evidently!"

"Flaunting your lordly title again?"

Byron's eyes flashed fire through their long drooping lashes, and the colour rose high in his cheeks: then he relaxed and laughed, sardonically this time. "Oh, that abominable Review! And how abominable of you to remind me of it. Admit that my lordly title is serving us well at present, and has done."

Hobhouse put a hand to his friend's shoulder, and shook it.

"I do, I do, and thank you for it. I think myself very well placed here on the strength of it."

Byron sat down and nodded. "Yes," he said, "think of it! In our own civilized England who would – nay, who *could* command a man to prepare his house for the reception of two complete strangers from heaven knows where *and* be obeyed? Which of our illustrious potentates would take their charge upon himself of his own volition and be offended at the thought of payment? Portland?"

Solid Whig that he was, Hobhouse grinned at the gibe. Hands dug deep in his pockets, Byron spoke thoughtfully. "So! My lordly title, if flaunted circumspectly, will bring me rewards far from home which my own begrudge me. It galls me, John, it galls me! They sneered at my poetry, bless you, because I never lived in a garret but had the sway of Newstead Abbey. Their very words – their very words. I should have invited them all to eat those words at Newstead, shouldn't I? No garret could have been more Spartan! Newstead is bigger, that is all, and noble-men are not necessarily strangers to poverty. Well! My tenant left me a ruin and much of it must stay so: but now that I have lived there I know that it is a part of me and I a part of its very fabric. I love it, John, I love it. I can endure privation for its good: I have fixed my heart on it and we stand or fall together. An Englishman's home is his castle, John: the lowest peasant feels the same for his cottage: but my cottage is an Abbey, so therefore I cannot be a poet. I do not see the argument but I am assured it must be so! But I will show them – I will show them all!"

The door opened, and their Greek host poked his nose in: breakfast had been prepared, would his noble visitors refresh themselves? They would: indeed they would! Both young men found themselves suddenly ravenous, and Byron, who wished to learn all he could, requested *Signor* Nicolo to join them.

"The *Signorio* do me too much honour – I am not worthy of such condescension."

All this fulsome humility was getting to be too much of a good thing – Mylord became impatient.

"Come, come, enough of that! We are your grateful tenants and besides, I want to talk to you. Sit down, man! Here's coffee all round so loosen your tongue and tell me how you come to be called *Signor* and how you speak, thank God! Italian."

Nicolo smiled, sat as he was bidden and answered, "It is true, Mylord, that I am a true Greek and a good Greek but I have spent several years in Trieste and for that they have nicknamed me the *Signor*. When the Governor of Malta wrote to warn – no, not warn, *advise* – the Pasha of your coming, he adjudged my house the most suitable for your reception and myself best fitted to entertain you."

"He has excellent judgement. But then a man of his position would need it."

"He is a very mighty Pasha indeed," said Nicolo.

Byron frowned. "Do you admire him?"

"As all men must."

"Do you – er – resent him?"

Nicolo knit his brows. "Resent? Why? I do not understand?"

"I think you do. You are a Greek – a descendant of a great and ancient culture – possibly of the greatest the world has ever known. The Pasha is a Turk – and Turkey reigns supreme. I repeat – do you resent him?"

Nicolo rolled his eyes and a look of the utmost alarm spread over his sallow cheeks.

"You speak of ages past, Mylord – that is for the history books. Albania and Greece have been Turkish these three-four hundred years and we remember only in legend."

"But do you not crave freedom?"

"Freedom? Eleutheria? A great, grand word, Mylord – but I am free enough. I have my home, my living: I am answerable to none but the law – what else should a man crave?"

Byron shook his head slowly. "I do not know," he admitted, "but for the sons of Leonidas to submit to the sons of Islam."

Nicolo interrupted him. "Do not imagine that Islam is not courteous and tolerant as long as the law is obeyed. We Greeks, for instance, are not bound by the Crescent – that ended at Lepanto! We have our own Church, our own Archbishop – indeed," he chuckled, "you have met the Primate yourselves, for he was here under this roof this very morning."

Hobhouse, who had been on the fret and anxious to change the tone of a dangerous conversation, let out a whoop of laughter. "No! The silent priest! The little man with the big hat! George, we must hasten to repay our respects. We did not realise, *Signor*, that he was so important a man. And really, George, I think it most unbecoming of you to criticize the Pasha when he insists on such bounteous entertainment. You are sensible of it yourself – you have said so!"

"True – I stand corrected. He has made most comfortable arrangements for us and I'm not ungrateful." He smiled his sweet smile at his troubled-looking host. "Truly, we appreciate all that you are doing for us. Such sights as we must have seemed when we arrived after our drenching ride! And how good it was to sleep once more in a bed! And without a pistol at my pillow! You cannot conceive how different from our previous night's lodging!"

"Oh, can I not? I have seen some of our country hans* – sampled them too, in my time. They are for the young and intrepid indeed! May I ask where Mylord laid his head?"

"At St. Dimetre. It had a very good stable – the horses at least were well housed. Our own loft was certainly cosy – seven men crowded in where the three of us were already sufficient – and at least one of them had very odd personal habits!" He chuckled. "Imagine to yourself a stuffy stable-loft where a couple of surly fellows with pistols muttered and grumbled and glared at us in the lamplight. It was cold, but we couldn't light a fire for fear of setting light to the place. We were thankful for the presence of a priest among us, believe me – we felt a measure of security with this man of peace but took care to keep our weapons at hand and slept but fitfully." His shoulders began to shake. "Poor man! He couldn't help his surly looks but Fletcher was horrified by his morning toilet. Gargling and spitting to clean himself inside and spinning like a dervish to blow the air through his

---

* Small wayside self-catering shelter

limbs outside did not amuse Fletcher. He is, you see, very fastidious in his own person!"

Hobhouse was grinning at the memory: Nicolo smiled through his moustachios. "And you, Mylord?"

"Oh, I'm not nearly so nice. But my poor Fletcher will never forgive me, I fear. However, he dared not grumble: I have promised to send him back in a transport if he does not behave himself. He's a dull dog – I believe there is no spirit of adventure in him at all!"

"Be fair, George – he has been sorely tried keeping our traps together and with the two of us to look after. He has performed wonders in very unaccustomed surroundings – he even managed boiled eggs for our supper!"

"Oh, he's a faithful fellow. I hope his breakfast has been as good as ours. Tell him, *Signor*, if you would be so good, to bring round the horses – we're off to see the sights!"

Iannina was all fascination to both young pairs of English eyes. Everything about it was new, different, barbaric. The glittering domes of mosque and house, reflected in the no less glittering waters of the lake, sparkled in the hard sunlight that had succeeded yesterday's downpour: oranges and lemons glowed like lamps in the suburban gardens, set off by the darkly green cypress groves and the grey background of the rocky mountain rising sharply above the waters. The two friends pushed their horses through the teeming street, bounded on one side by the tombstones of the Turkish dead and on the other by the commerce of the living. The living thronged the street, the sellers and the buyers, picturesque and a world removed from sedate, decorous England. As in England, the women wore skirts to their ankles, but they were full and wide, not clinging to the figure: they topped their gowns with laced-up bodices or small sleeveless jackets, their shoes curled up at the toes, and under their little round hats a scarf fell, covering the backs of their necks – a sensible precaution under this hotter sun. As for the men, they too wore the round hat but without the scarf, and many had tossed a sheepskin over their shoulders to enhance the aura of wildness they, the sons of Tamburlane, carried with them: and like their womenfold they too favoured a flowing style below the waist, binding their baggy trousers Saxon-fashion with strips of cloth. In the bazaar, the Englishmen exclaimed aloud at the richness of the wares, at the splendid silver and gold embroideries hanging out for sale – Byron determined that his sister should receive at least one sumptuous scarf on his return. It would suit her stately beauty to perfection.

He sighed to himself. Dear Augusta! He wondered what she was doing at this moment – was she perhaps thinking of him and wondering what *he* was about? He could imagine her so well: sitting in her pretty morning-room, perhaps consulting her housekeeper: but she – no, she could have no notion of the exotic sights and sounds surrounding him, sights and sounds of which she would only read in books – or, more likely, from his letters. High time she had one, or she would forget him altogether. His smile deepened. As if she would! Or *could*! Half siblings only, they might have been twins, so strong was the bond that held them. And she had married her Dragoon colonel – a dull dog if ever he'd met one! Had been married these two full years. Was she happy? He supposed so – hoped so, for her sake and his own. When her first child, a daughter, was born, he had written to her with fraternal carelessness. "I return to you my best thanks for making me an uncle, and forgive the sex this time, but the next *must* be a nephew ..." Yet Augusta understood his pride in his new status and his relief at her safety, which he would not publicly express. It was high time she had a letter from him.

Lost in thought as he was, he insensibly became aware that behind them, Fletcher was keeping up a permanent grumble. The heat, the smells, the underlying savagery upset his sensibilities. Bond Street was one thing – it pleased him to send his master upon the strut looking point-de-vice. Here there was no outlet for his professional talents. Even the haunted dilapidation of Newstead was tolerable: his lordship's ancestral seat must reflect honour upon his lordship's valet. But this – this fair gave him the shudders. Look at the unhealthy habits of these barbarians! Why, there was a joint of meat hanging, if you please, right out in the open, from a tree, instead of in the butcher's shop anigh it. He pointed this out to Hobhouse, who, after a startled look, turned green and averted his gaze.

"Don't look, George!" he begged. "It's a man's arm – wrenched from the socket!"

Fletcher gasped. "Sir!" he exclaimed. "It is – it IS an arm! Are they cannibals, too, in this place?"

True enough, a brawny arm dangled by a string from its fingers – had the string been six inches longer, it would have knocked off a tall rider's hat. Part of the flank remained attached to what had been the armpit. Already, the maggots were wriggling obscenely among the sinews. A slight breeze had sprung up, and Byron hastily put his handkerchief to his nose.

And this, they were to learn, was the summary justice in a rough land, beheading and dismemberment being the fate of robbers under Islamic law.

"An effective punishment," commented Byron, when later they passed the blackened and infested head. "It would be a consummate rogue indeed who is undeterred by such a sight. Perhaps, John, we are not so far removed from Hellas as I thought. I think this is a fair legacy from Sinis the Pinebender – don't you think so?"

"I'm trying not to think at all – in fact, I think I've had enough. I shall go back to Nicolo's for a siesta – will you come?"

"Yes, I'll come. And tomorrow we'll do the polite and pay our respects to the Bey!"

***

"I think I shall flaunt my title," Byron said thoughtfully over next morning's breakfast, as they prepared to visit the Bey. "Here it seems to be appreciated, if not at home."

"Oh, George!" cried Hobhhouse, in exasperation. "Can't you forget it for one moment? Does it go so deep?"

His lordship smiled, a sudden smile of singular sweetness.

"I suppose it must do," he said. "Strange. I had thought I no longer cared. It's all your fault – you reminded me of it yesterday."

"Mea culpa," grinned his friend. "But in all seriousness I feel you may be right. These people have treated us with honour and it would never do to offend them."

"Quite so! So – our best apparel, and I will wear my sword. *Noblesse oblige!*"

"Come then, Mylord! The horses await!"

Byron aimed a mock punch at him: Hobhouse feinted in the same style: and, laughing, they went out of the house to the waiting horses. The morning was fresh: likewise the horses, and Byron, who was never renowned for his horsemanship, drew a breath of relief as they alighted in the palace courtyard. His mount had shied violently at a ragged beggar crouching by the gate: it would never have done to have landed ignominiously at the feet of the guide who came in state to greet them. He wished he could have dismounted with the careless grace he envied in other men – but the cursed lameness of which he was so conscious prevented him. He knew the man had noticed his infirmity: he saw the quick flash of interested compassion in the dark eyes: but with innate courtesy the flunkey bowed with bent head and spread hands, and motioned them to follow him into the presence of the young Bey. The very young Bey: all of ten years old, this grandson of the Pasha, composed beyond his years and totally unembarrassed by his distinguished visitors. He smiled, bowed, and indicated with a gesture that they should sit near to him, while a grave old man with a long white beard that reached to his knees nodded silent approval. Had they not known that the Pasha was sixty miles away, the travellers might well have mistaken his identity, but it appeared that he was the Preceptor, well-pleased with his young master's performance. Byron's instinct had not led him astray: the boy was fascinated by the handsome sword girt about his lordship's middle. The thin ice of convention was easily broken as the descendant of a warrior race fingered the weapon which Byron good-naturedly unbuckled for his closer inspection.

"You have fine craftsmen in your country, Mylord," the boy remarked enviously. "So very fine a blade!"

Byron smiled. "Swords, yes, and gunsmiths too. Our weapons of war and destruction are second to none."

The Bey nodded gravely. "Yours is a warlike race," he said, "and well esteemed by men such as we." Hobhouse smiled to himself. The child continued, "It is a great honour that you do us, to come so far to seek us out. My grandfather left orders that you should be treated with all courtesy. I trust our people have obeyed them well?"

"We are most comfortably lodged, your Highness."

"It is well. Else there would be a reckoning." He clapped his hands, and a servant came to his knee, bowing low. "Refreshment for our honoured guests!" commanded the boy, and the familiar bitter coffee soon appeared, with sweetmeats of a singularly sticky nature. Hobhouse's amusement grew as the youthful Bey licked his fingers noisily. Byron wiped the sugar from his fingertips with the finest of cambric handkerchieves, at which the Bey opened his eyes wide.

"What is that?" he demanded, natural curiosity overcoming courtesy.

Byron explained with all due gravity the use of that necessary and useful adjunct to a gentleman's costume. The Bey nodded his understanding. "Your ways are very different from ours," he said. "Even your apparel sets you apart from us. We like our clothes to be loose and flowing for coolness – but yours are cut close to your form."

"Our country is far to the north," said Hobhouse, "and the sun is not so fierce."

The Bey digested this and was obviously about to make more pertinent comments but caught the warning eye of his aged mentor. He looked up and said instead, "Come! Why do we detain you in this poor apartment? Come and see my Palace, and you shall judge of what we have to show!"

He beckoned to the servant. "Send the women to the harem!" he ordered, much to Byron's disappointment. "We go to tour the Palace!" He rose and gestured to the two Englishmen, politely indicating that they should go before him along the gallery, pausing every few steps to view the paintings on the wainscots. Disappointingly, the attendant's progress had been swifter than their own: no veiled form flitted before them, no silvery laughter hit upon their straining ears. The harem hid its secrets well.

The rooms through which they were escorted were large and comfortably furnished in a surprisingly Western style. Comparing notes afterwards, the friends found that each had been expecting cold marble and cushions, but instead the most comfortable sofas covered in rich brocades like those in the bazaar invited repose, and even richer carpets covered some of the floors. These rooms, it was explained, were intended for winter use. In fact, the only marble they encountered was in a kind of bathroom set into a recess with its own fountain. Byron said under his breath, "This seems to me the height of sybaritism, John! So much for the dignity of Newstead!"

The Bey was delighted at their amazement, especially when Hobhouse congratulated him on the quality of the glass in the large, deep windows.

"Finest Venetian, upon my word!" he declared. Then doubtfully – "isn't it?"

"Of course. Our trade with the Adriatic states is constant and beneficial to all."

"But you do not curtain them?"

They Bey wrinkled his brow. "Curtains? They are for doorways."

"Yes, curtains. In England we drape our windows, and your beautiful fabrics would be highly prized for such use."

"Why do you do that?"

"For several reasons – to shade our furnishings from the light, to adorn the window and – to provide privacy from prying eyes."

"There are none such here," the Bey declared. "They would not dare! We would put out their spying eyes with hot vinegar!"

Remembering the rotting robber whose quarters decorated the streets through which they had come, his guests could well believe it. But every saloon, handsome though it was, appeared to be for daytime use. Curiously, they enquired about sleeping quarters. The Bey was boyishly delighted.

"We sleep where we wish – where it happens to be convenient!" he crowed. "See!" and opening a cupboard he showed it piled with bedding. "Why set apart a chamber for sloth?" he demanded. "Is it indeed so in England? That is strange indeed!"

They had seen all that was permitted to be seen, but the Bey was loath to let them go. "We shall go to visit my kinsman!" he said. "He will not thank me if you do not taste also of his hospitality." He clapped his hands again: orders flew. "Go to Veli Pasha's palace and tell them of our approach," he cried. "Go saddle my horse, and those of these my honoured guests! Go summon our escort!" and before many moments had passed they were out once more amid the throng. The beggar still whined at the gateway: the noises, the smells, the shouts were the same: but this time there was no need to push their horses through the press of people or fend off the importunity of the sweetmeat sellers. The crowd parted as if by magic: the passers-by bowed low, so low that they could touch the ground with their right hands before bringing them to mouth and brow in salute. The Bey received this homage gravely, inclining his head and laying his right hand on his breast. In the true spirit, so it seemed, of Gothic romance, the procession galloped across the Palace courtyard to where the Bey's kinsman waited to embrace him. The formalities began again – pipes were offered, the inevitable coffee, the grand tour of the apartments. It was all too much for the even more youthful host, whose seven-year-old legs began to itch at this stately progress. Much to the visitors' amusement he began to skip along the gallery, but before he had executed more than a couple of steps the Bey's brown hand shot out and grabbed his shoulder. "Walk more quietly!" he commanded. "Recollect that you are in the presence of strangers!" The child ceased his prancing on the instant, and the distinguished strangers caught each other's glance across his head. Each was thinking how any normal English boy would have slid from end to end of that polished floor: each was impressed by the dignity of these children, so conscious of their rank and the duty they owed to it. Each felt profoundly sorry for them, middle-aged even in childhood. It was all so very strange – had they expected otherwise? and yet so very like. The tattered bundle of bones that crouched by the palace gate – was it so very far removed from the reeking slums of Westminster? The indifference of the crowd to the dismembered corpse exposed about the town – was it so different from the filthy cells of Newgate where (Byron's imagination shuddered) but for the grace of God either one of them could be condemned? If savagery here seemed obvious, was it so very far beneath the surface in civilized England? And the near vulgarity of the Pasha's palaces was reflected in the grand saloons of every wealthy city merchant. It was a sobering thought.

Late that night Hobhouse, climbing the stairs after sitting up later than his companion, saw a line of light under Byron's door. He tapped softly on the panels: then, getting no reply, pushed it gently open and peeped in. His lordship was sitting at the table, scribbling furiously in the lamplight. Hobhouse withdrew as softly as he had entered: Byron never raised his head. His fingers flew over the paper. He was not writing a letter to his sister. He was out to prove himself.

***

During the next few days, the pattern was repeated. The Vizier's horses would be brought round for their use and the friends would set out to explore the wild and picturesque country seen by so few of their compatriots. The immense lake divided, as it seemed, the civilized from the untamed, with gardens and groves on the city shore and on the other a chain of mountains, their tops hidden from view by the morning mist. On one day their way took them over a bridge and a long ride towards the monastery of St. Elias: on another day along the course of the river some claimed to be Acheron: on yet another across the plain to the ancient amphitheatre of stone with its rising rows of high seats. Byron was enchanted. This alone was worth the long, hot, physically uncomfortable ride. Hobhouse had led the way, clambering up the stone steps and seating himself so as to view the theatre as a whole: but when he turned to address some laughing remark he found himself alone. Then he heard his friend's voice and saw him down below the auditorium, head thrown back, arms raised. "See you," he called, "some place to sit in the sacred grove or on the common land? There let me rest, what time we find our situation. John, John, do you hear me? Do you hear me and Oedipus? Yes, I see you do – wait there for me!"

Every word was clear from the distant figure down below, who came clambering clumsily but eagerly up, impatient of the limping step that slowed his progress.

"**Could** you hear me?"

"Very clearly. What wonderful architects these old fellows were! I declare I never heard so well at Drury Lane."

"This is marvellous. And what **is** our situation, now we have found a place to sit? Can this be Epirus, as some say? And now neglected, ruined, grown over, all those voices stilled for ever. The barbarians have conquered, John, and if the true heirs returned tomorrow this heritage would still be desolate."

"I do not think," said Hobhouse in his calming way, "that nineteenth century man would sit outdoors to hear the play – not without cushions." He rose, ruefully rubbing himself to make George laugh. "No, but only think," he said, as they made their way back to where the horses were tethered, quietly cropping among the ancient ruins. "If the ghosts of the departed still walk that stage, how they must reproach their descendants! What must they think, to see Mahmood dethrone Zeus and their shrines fall into decay? If Sophocles had had prophetic power, what a tragedy he could have brought upon this stage! And no one would believe it."

"Instead of which," remarked Hobhouse, "we have not an ancient prophet but The Prophet – and that is unworthy of me!"

But gentlemen can only spend so much time in one place without becoming restless, and it was in many ways a relief when word came from the Secretary that, his accounts now having been prepared for the Pasha's inspection, he was ready to accompany and sustain the noble visitors on the journey northward. Byron went to supervise the grumbling Fletcher as he assembled the luggage. It looked impressive enough. Four large trunks, three smaller trunks, the beds, bedding and the indispensable canteen ought to reflect their noble situation, he thought. The packhorses grunted and grumbled as each load went into the panniers: Fletcher grumbled and cursed the clumsiness of the Albanians: Nicolo's moustachios drooped as the moment of departure drew nearer.

"Ah, Mylord!" he sighed. "I shall remember to my life's end the honour you have paid my house. I would you might return."

Byron held out his hand and shook the other's with feeling. "I would I might," he said, softly. "I would I might. But I shall never forget." Then with shouting and grumbling and a clink of iron shoes the little procession passed between the lemon trees in the courtyard, through the folding doors and away down the street on the ride northward to Tepellene and Ali Pasha.

In its way, it was quite impressive. At the head rode Vasilly, the Albanian soldier of the City Guard who had been allotted the task of protecting and seeing to the comfort of the noble travellers. Behind him came the noble travellers themselves, followed closely by the Secretary and one of his relations, a man in holy orders who was faced with the uncomfortable task of explaining to the Pasha why his taxes were overdue. After them came the packhorses, and bringing up the rear the resigned Fletcher. Waved on their way by half the populace of Iannina, they crossed the wide defensive ditch outside the city and set off across the plain northward, eagerly assimilating a whole new range of sights and smells. To one side the hills were topped by ruined walls and to the left a line of tents attracted Byron's attention.

"Hi, Vasilly," he called. "Come here a minute, there's a good fellow!"

Vasilly galloped back. "Mylord?" he asked.

"Tell me, Vasilly, who are these nomads, camping in the vineyards?"

"They are no nomads, Mylord. They belong to those who tend the harvest; when the grapes are ready, the people move out from the villages and stay here until the work is done. Thus the work is uninterrupted, and all is secure from robbers." He smiled with satisfaction. "This year the harvest will be good," he declared. "There will be much wine of a strength fit for warriors. All due precaution must be taken."

"Then I wish," said Byron, "we had come a month or so later. I'm as dry as a bone."

"I rather think," put in Hobhouse, "that you won't say that much longer. Look at those clouds! It's going to rain before long."

"I think you're right. The devil! We could do without that. Then, let's push on."

"Not too fast, Mylord – the ground is marshy and a man must take care where he places the soles of his feet. It is for this reason that the Pasha has ordered bridges to be built: else there would be no passage in bad weather."

Sure enough, from time to time the travellers passed small groups of workmen labouring to make crossing places over the worst of the marsh: to them Vasilly would shout a greeting, the Secretary would throw a piastre or two, and the procession would go over with much shouting and a touching of caps. Once, a man bolder and more inquisitive than his fellows called, "Who be ye? Why do ye seek passage?" and was answered, "To the

Pasha, by his command and invitation." It was enough – the man fell silently to work once more.

They pushed on through the grey afternoon. The dusk was gathering fast – so were the storm clouds: Byron pulled up his coat collar and rode in gloomy silence. The marsh seemed interminable, but at least the road across it had been well made, which was more than could be said for the occasional homesteads along the way. Byron had suffered a severe shock when the Secretary came up to him, coughed deprecatingly, and drew his attention to a poor-looking building atop a crag overlooking the road. "Mylord, you visited Hussein Bey at the palace in Iannina – yonder is the home of his affianced bride."

Byron was staggered, partly by the youth of the intending bridegroom but also by the mean appearance of his father-in-law's home, far removed from the opulence he had deplored to himself within the palace. The Secretary read his look correctly. "You must not think, Mylord, that Hussein Bey demeans himself by this match – the Pasha insists on the highest nobility for his sons and grandsons. Here in the wilder parts of our beloved country the Turk cares little for grand dwellings, but the girl's dowry is fair enough, be very sure."

"**Our** beloved country?" thought Byron to himself. "Whose? The Turks? Ali Pasha's? or the country of Alexander?"

The threatened rain had started to fall: weeping, thought Byron, in a flight of morbid fancy, for the lost gods of Olympus. Huddled into his great turned-up collar, he merely nodded when the Secretary excused himself and rode ahead. They had come to the edge of the marsh, where a miserable travellers' rest stood – so mean that it was decided to pass it by and carry on along a stony pass through the low hills that succeeded the marshland till the village should be reached. Night was falling fast: it was soon very dark, and the rain, which had been steadily gathering in intensity, was coming down in torrents. Hobhouse, his hat pulled low upon his brows, head bent against the force of the wind, urged his tired horse where Vasilly led, shutting his ears to the continual tut-tutting of the Secretary. Slipping and sliding along the narrow lanes, he realised after a hundred years, or so it seemed, that they had stopped outside some kind of shelter. It was too dark to see properly, but he slid gratefully down from his sodden horse and entered, leading the jaded animal behind him.

Vasilly was already busy inside, lighting a fire whose smoke had no other outlet but the door. An oil lamp glowed in the dark: Hobhouse found by its light rings at one end of the hovel where the horses could be tethered, and set about making them comfortable. The steam that rose from their flanks did nothing to help the general dankness, but they seemed contented enough, gently lipping at a heap of fodder in a corner.

"Come sir, come!" cried the Secretary. "Repose yourself a little! We can go no further and do no more this night."

"Where's Vasilly?"

"Gone into the village for food: he will be here in a little moment. Hark! Hark to the wind! God is good, to bring us under a roof in this night. Sit, sir, sit! In a little while we shall sup all together."

He had spread a carpet from his pack on the mud floor of the hut beside the infant fire, and patted it invitingly.

"Where is Mylord?" began Hobhouse, but his words were drowned in an unholy shriek as the wind screamed overhead. "Where is Mylord?" he cried: at which moment Vasilly staggered through the doorway, blown in, it seemed, his pockets bulging with what proved to be some tiny eggs and with four scrawny fowls dangling from his hands.

"Not yet arrived," he panted, dropped the corpses on the floor and shaking the water from him like a dog. "He cannot be far behind: he took charge of the servants and the baggage, and their beasts are slow. He will most surely be here what time supper is ready." And taking an evil-looking knife from his belt he began to dismember and disembowel the chickens with the utmost composure and skill.

Time passed: the thunder which had been growling in the distance for some time now crashed overhead, peal upon peal, rolling round the mountains in a trapped frenzy and trying desperately to escape above them. The rain lashed down pitilessly. Hobhouse, peering through the cracks in the wooden planking that formed the walls of the shelter, could see the hilltops dazzlingly silhouetted as the lightning flashed viciously and, it seemed, incessantly. In the distance he could hear the weeping of women and the voices of men calling upon god to spare them. Even so, he thought, must their ancestors have called upon Zeus for protection against his thunderbolts: he seemed transported out of time into a stranger, more primitive world. The horses shivered and tossed their heads: the Secretary placidly ate a boiled egg: but Hobhouse was in the fidgets, restlessly pacing up and down, half out of his mind with anxiety.

"Do not worry so," urged the Secretary. "The guides know every part of this country as well as the backs of their hands, and Mylord has also his own faithful servant with him. They have found shelter in the village, beyond doubt – they can have come to no harm there. You will see! Lie down and rest, sir: you can do no good by all this prowling."

But Hobhouse could not rest. The cold, dark hours were passing: he could not sit and do nothing. He beckoned Vasilly to him.

"They *must* be lost!" he said to him. "And who could survive such a tempest? We must do *something!*" Vasilly shrugged. He knew the violence of the local climate and was fatalistic by nature.

"What would you have me do?" he demanded. "We cannot search in the dark – we must wait until morning."

Hobhouse nearly danced with impatience, but his mind caught the one word, "dark".

"Light!" he cried. "Light! That is what we must do! Come, call the men we have with us and light fires on the hilltop – if Mylord sees that he will at least know where we are! And fire a gun – two guns – all the guns we have! We must attract his notice – he *cannot* be so very far behind!"

A tremendous crash immediately overhead drowned his voice. Vasilly shrugged again. It should be as the Englishman wished – his words would be a command – but in his opinion there was too much noise and light going on anyway for their poor efforts to be of use. He had heard that the English were a race of madmen – now he believed it. But the orders were given: other leaping flames joined the lightning flashes and a tinny pop-pop-pop echoed the thunder's roll. Hobhouse lay down as he was in his damp greatcoat: he could not sleep, but the small comfort of having taken some action, however useless, had calmed his mind somewhat. Even if he had not been worried almost to death he could not have slept – the thunder, the lashing of the rain, the shouting of men, the barking of the village curs and the Secretary's snoring would have seen to that. He rolled restlessly on the Secretary's carpet. "Oh George, George!" he muttered, "Where the devil are you?"

Had he known, he would have been by no means easier in his mind. Having fallen behind with the slower-moving baggage animals Byron, trusting in the boasted local knowledge of the guides, had followed meekly where they led. His main concern had been to withstand the force of the wind. When the first flash of lightning had caused his horse to rear he had had difficulty in retaining his seat: having got the animal under control, he realised that the whole party had stopped and that the guides were having a furious argument. This was conducted in the local dialect, but though he couldn't understand a word he gathered the gist of it and recognised it as stirring stuff.

"Son of a dishwasher! Did I not say we should turn left instead of right? Do we know this crag? Where are the Pasha's men and the honourable gentlemen?"

"How should I know? They are not here."

"Where is here?"

"How should I know that either? *Thou* art in charge."

"I? I?" The voice rose to a scream. "Who was it cried that he alone could lead us right? Thou shouldst be left to beg thy bread at the gates of Iannina with other blind men!"

"Mylord, Mylord! What shall we do? What are those men saying?"

"For God's sake, Fletcher, don't *you* start. I don't know what's happened but I imagine we've taken a wrong turn in the dark. We'd best make a back cast to the place where the path seemed to divide – we'll try the other one and see what happens. We've reached a dead end here so in any case we can't go forward. Hi! Stop that noise and come here at once!"

The two guides stopped arguing as one at the sound of his voice: the younger came to his stirrup and asked, "What is Mylord's desire?"

"Mylord desires that you turn about with him and seek to find that which is lost – in other words, the way! Come!" and he wheeled his horse about leaving no room for argument. "Come along, Fletcher!" he called into the wind. "Let's waste no more time here," and set off back down the way they had come, leaving the cavalcade to follow as best it might. It was difficult enough to find the path and the scene through which they had just passed was repeated, with variations, until a more than vivid flash showed them to be following the brink of a raging stream tumbling along some way below, and surrounded by macabre stones which had certainly not been placed there by nature. Yells of superstitious fear from the guides told Byron where they were, or rather, in what kind of place, for their actual location was a mystery to him and the self-styled experts seemed to be no wiser. Despite the wet, the cold and his chattering teeth, he began to laugh.

"A graveyard!" he called to Fletcher, following dismally at his heels. "A graveyard as I live – or maybe die – and if I die, what better place to save time and trouble! Come, Fletcher, we must find what poor shelter we can here, and surely these poor shades won't grudge us that much comfort."

"If it's all the same to you, Mylord," said Fletcher morosely, as he caught the stiff and sodden bridle, "I'd as lief not stay here – it fair gives me the creeps."

"Nonsense, man, it won't hurt you! And I'm of the opinion that we shall be safer with the ancient dead than staggering along the bank in this storm. At least we may come out of the wind if we crouch against a tombstone apiece. What the devil's that?"

Behind them, a fresh altercation had arisen – the guides, it seemed, would not desecrate the "han" of the dead by bivouacking among them. They shouted, the thunder rolled, and above it all rose the voice of George the dragoman, thoroughly enraged by the incompetence which had brought the party to such a pass.

"Fools! Cowards! If you fear to find death among the dead then you shall surely find it at my hands, thou cursed of Allah!" and a nearer explosion even than the thunder sounded close at hand as he fired off both his pistols, narrowly missing the unfortunate guides. He was shaking with impotent rage: the guides, shaking with fear, took to their heels and ran: Mylord shook with laughter: and Fletcher screamed out loud.

"Shots, Mylord! shots! There are brigands – hiding among the graves!"

"Rubbish, man – in *this* weather? All good brigands are snug indoors and I would that I were one of them! Oh dear, oh dear, my sides are aching and why I'm laughing I'm sure I've no idea!"

"Nor I, Mylord," answered Fletcher with some asperity. "I fail to see any humour in this situation. God in heaven!" as a brighter flash than any yet lit up the whole scene in brilliant relief. It showed Byron leaning, pale-faced and diverted, against his chosen monument: the patient priest, who all this while had meekly followed where he was led, frantically telling his beads in the lee of another: George the dragoman standing sheepishly holding his empty pistols: the remaining servants cowering: the wild-eyed horses: and the boiling torrent falling over itself as the downpour added to its waters. The sound of running feet had faded in the distance, but Mylord sensibly reflected that the party could hardly be more lost without their guides than they had been with them. He wondered idly how Hobhouse was faring: he would be beside himself with worry, Byron felt sure.

By this time Hobhouse was indeed in a fever of anxiety. It was past midnight and the storm still raged with unbridled ferocity. At any minute he expected the roof of the hovel where they lay to fly off and leave them all exposed to the deluge: he had almost determined to brave the storm and go in search himself when a fresh commotion began. Into the shelter, dripping from every stitch, rushed a wild figure that looked frantically round in the gloom, spied the Secretary and knelt panting at his side, pulling at his arm as if he would drag it from its socket.

The Secretary had fallen into a doze but at this rough treatment he started awake and found himself face to face with a countenance as pale and damp as a drowned man, and it took several minutes to convince him that in fact he was not dreaming this particular nightmare. Hobhouse, almost dancing with impatience, could make out only that someone or something had fallen down, and in his turn grabbed the Secretary's other arm. But the Secretary's aplomb had returned – likewise his loquacity.

"Have no more fear, sir – all is well!" he beamed. "Alas, Mylord has not found shelter as I had assured myself, still, all is well!

The way was mistaken in the dark, that is all, but now we know where he is and he shall be retrieved with all speed."

"All well!" gasped Hobhouse, appalled, "without shelter all these hours in *this*! I've never known a storm like it! I wish he may not have contracted a dangerous chill, or a fever. This is an unhealthy country, upon my word! Let us set out at once – at once – to bring him to safety."

"Let us not be too rash," answered the Secretary. "You are not used, Effendi, to these wild conditions. We shall send those who *are*, and you and I will prepare a little supper against his coming."

"If you haven't eaten all the eggs, certainly!"

This shaft fell on deaf ears – the Secretary was busily giving orders.

Hobhouse had to admit to himself that the fussy little man could be surprisingly efficient when necessary – the Pasha obviously did know what he was doing, after all. Rapidly he assembled ten men who knew the district well and sent them with fresh horses to the graveyard: overriding any superstitious reluctance with threats, promises and a further party whose torches of blazing pine would defy the downpour and any malignant spirits: and dispatching them into the night. The night seemed never-ending to one who stayed within the shelter but at last his straining ears caught the sounds for which he had been waiting and it was not long after that that a drenched and weary figure came limping into the hut.

Hobhouse leaped up, hand outstretched. "George! Thank God you're safe! Get those wet clothes off, man, and come to the fire! Tell us what happened! You are chilled to the bone!"

"I am uncertain of my role," answered Byron, "for I have been playing Lear these last eight hours and more, biding the pelting of the pitiless storm: but now, behold me transformed into Ophelia, for too much of water have I!" and his lordship, wringing his hat like a dishcloth, generously spattered his friend. "I fear it will take more than these 'paly flames' to dry me, but we must hope for the best. At least here there are the living for company."

Hobhouse's curiosity was by now aroused in earnest, but his relief at his friend's safety overbore it and he waited patiently while Mylord's wet boots were prized off – not without some difficulty – and until his supper was in his hands. Between mouthfuls, Byron described his adventure, leaving Hobhouse by turns dismayed, wrathful and consumed with mirth at his droll description of the graveyard farce.

"You can laugh," said Byron, "but upon my word I don't know that I can blame the poor fellows, apart from losing the way in the first place. Fletcher, now, is a different proposition."

The valet was affronted. "I, Mylord?"

"Yes, you, Fletcher! Our dignity was sadly undermined by you setting up such a screech. Next time I'll bring a lady's maid along with me. Never mind! We are all met in this Arcadian spot and while life and limb are safe who can ask for more? Where *are* we, John? Presumably this village has a name, poor but its own."

"It is called Zitza – or so I'm told."

"Zitza! Well, I shall remember it, whatever else I may forget of our tour. Tomorrow we'll have a look at it by daylight, not lightning flash. Goodnight now – or do I mean good morning?" And rolling himself in a dry blanket, Mylord fell instantly into the sleep of the exhausted.

***

Zitza next morning in the sunlight was very different from Zitza in drenching darkness. Byron had slept late and would have slept longer if a shocking row had not broken out just outside the shelter. He stretched, yawned, and strolled out to find a heated altercation in progress between Vasilly and the Greek guides, who with much gesture and loud justification were conducting a defence of their behaviour. To Byron's shocked amusement Vasilly, losing patience, raised his whip to them, whereupon they retreated, still shrilly grumbling, to a safe distance.

Vasilly turned, saw his noble employer steadily regarding him, and came cheerfully to greet him.

"Mylord is rested. Good! Now you will stay with Vasilly and all shall be well. These animals," – he waved his hand vaguely at the recent combatants – "need a soldier like myself to enforce discipline. Else, all is in chaos. They talk much – but when there are deeds to be done they are poltroons all. Indeed, the Pasha has much to vex him. Has Mylord taken his breakfast?"

Mylord had not. Mylord would be pleased to do so: and in a very few moments sat down to a pilaf of buttered rice and the remaining eggs. The weather was dry and fine after the storm, so that Byron, pinching himself to prove that last night's adventure really had happened, was eager enough to accompany the Secretary's party on his duty visits. The view on all sides was stupendous, for Zitza, like its neighbour villages, was not only situated on a steep hillside, but surrounded by wooded mountains: while below them the slope descended to the vineyards and the grazing grounds filled with sheep. The party climbed up one of these green hills and through a fine grove of oaks, surprisingly English in its appearance, to the main village. Here everything was Greek, not Albanian, and the chief building, to which the Secretary led the way with some pomposity, was the Christian monastery.

He marched purposefully up to the door, and banged a summons on its battered iron plates which bore silent testimony to former assaults by robber bands. "I laughed at poor Fletcher," thought Byron to himself, "but it would seem that his fears were not without foundation."

The grating slid back and a rheumy eye peered out. "Who calls?"

"The Inspector of the Pasha. Open up!"

"It is not time."

"The Pasha chooses his own time. Open, I say!"

"Wait there. I must consult the Papa."

The Secretary danced with impatience.

"Open, I say! Open to the Inspector of Ali Pasha! Shall I believe you have that within that is to be concealed? Open!"

The eye disappeared, and a disgruntled muttering could be heard on the other side of the door: then a grating noise as the key was slowly turned and the door was slowly swung open, its ancient hinges protesting mightily. The aged custodian counted them in and would doubtless count them out again: and the Prior, hearing unaccustomed voices, hurried out to meet them full of the most humble apologies. He was a meek little man whom the Secretary would obviously find it easy enough to bully. Byron believed that the refreshment offered them was brought in all sincerity and not as a bribe: the little man was clearly over-awed by his company and ushered them into his own room, where a fire was burning. Mylord was glad to edge his way close to the glowing logs – he could still feel last night's chill in his bones. But the warmth, the fruit and an amazingly soft white wine all helped to dismiss the sensation. He praised the wine sincerely, marvelling at its quality. The Prior's face brightened.

"Mylord approves? It is our very own vintage from our very own grapes."

"But are they different from the others grown in these parts?"

"By no means! they are the same, but the secret is in the process thereof. We do not tread our grapes coarsely with our feet, trampling them so that they bruise and crush and cry for mercy. We press them gently, so gently, with our hands: and again and yet again, so that the lifeblood is yielded graciously and all bitterness is removed. I hope Mylord will accept some for his own use and to remember us?"

Mylord had a better idea. "If you will permit, Father, I will accept your offer very readily and ask you another favour beside. We are on our way to pay our respects to the Pasha: when we return, will your monastery afford us a lodging? Our shelter last night was shelter, no more: if you could see your way to housing us, you would not lose thereby."

The Prior was glad to close with this proposal: the Secretary frowned, began to speak and thought better of it. What Ali did not know would not trouble him: and his orders, after all, were to see that the English Mylord's whims were complied with for the greater honour of Albania. He made up for it when the time came to talk to the previous night's landlord.

The village headman, polite to a fault, had brought his accounts to be passed and signed. Byron disliked and distrusted him: his servility rang false, and he was suspected in his lordship's opinion of currying favour with the Pasha by contributing more to the Exchequer than his neighbours could fairly afford. The delegation that followed confirmed every suspicion: thin, ragged and disconsolate, they came to remonstrate with the Secretary with the hovel's owner as their spokesman.

The Secretary frowned portentously. Byron crooked his finger, and George the dragoman hurried over. "Mylord?"

"Tell me what this fellow is saying."

George nodded. He loved to show off his knowledge of English: and the English were generous when well-served. He listened attentively.

"You complain to me," said the Secretary, "that you cannot pay your taxes. That is mutiny – revolution! It is a serious thing that you say. How can you not pay? Your headman has assessed your means, and he knows you only too well. Cannot pay? *Will* not pay, more like!" He was working himself up into a rare passion.

"Sir, he has not considered! It is true that hereabouts the soil is rich and the flocks are numberless. But think – only think! The best and richest lands belong to the monastery, and the monastery pays no tax. Therefore we are taxed twice over, for ourselves and for the Fathers. It is very clear."

"It's clear to me that you are conniving rogues who would cheat the Pasha of his just dues. For that you shall pay twice over!"

The man threw out his hands imploringly. "Ah, no, no, only listen!"

"I will not! You are wasting my valuable time!"

Byron stepped forward. "Wait!" he said. "Let us hear what this poor man has to say. Indeed, I do not think him a rogue but an honest man who deserves to be heard for justice's sake."

The man looked eagerly at Byron. "Mylord is just! Only listen! We pay our fair taxes to the Government – that is but fair, and we do not quarrel with it. If that were all, we could live! But to pay the taxes of the monastery beside, we would have to sell all – all. Wine – corn – milk – flocks – all would go and leave us with nothing! There is food in plenty: but we would starve, for the food must be sold to pay these dues. We labour all day in vain: for we get no reward from it. We are asked to render 13,000 piastres to the Exchequer: and when that is done our wives and children will go naked and starving. It is cruel: and it is foolish, for when we are dead from cold and famine, who will then pay these taxes?"

That last plea appeared to strike the Secretary where the man's miserable appearance had left him unmoved: but Byron had been shocked by the whole. A quick calculation showed the demand to be in the nature of seven hundred pounds! He was appalled.

"Tell him," he said to the Secretary, "that I will myself discuss this matter with Ali Pasha when we meet, and ask him to reduce the levy."

The Secretary did as he was told, with obvious reluctance, and the man seized Byron's hand in both his own. Looking him straight in the eye he said, "Mylord, be very sure of our gratitude for ever. When a Greek owes thanks, he never forgets!"

The sound of his voice and the glow in his eye stayed with Byron as they made their way back down the slope. "And I will never forget!" he mused to himself. "Impoverished, proud and oppressed, I will never forget you. Something must be done! something *shall* be done!" And he looked forward even more keenly than before to his meeting with the Pasha.

Next day they set off again in the Pasha's wake. The journey followed much the same pattern, through valleys, over bridges that crossed rivers in spate (one the Secretary declared to be Acheron of old, but Byron doubted this), past groves and vineyards, overlooked by wooded hills. There was even another thunderstorm, and this second deluge made the going difficult in the extreme, even hazardous, with the baggage horses staggering and stumbling under their loads. Eventually they gave up trying and sought refuge with a local priest, a poor man who made them free of what little he had. Byron's brow grew dark as he heard once more the tale of extortion and repression attached to his indigent host. Here, it seemed, the whole village was the Pasha's private property: half of its produce was paid to him and everyone in it was subject to his orders in every detail of their lives.

"Upon my word," he muttered to Hobhouse when for a moment or two they were alone, "I am amazed that the peasantry have not risen in their wrath long since. It passes all belief!"

"Hush!" warned Hobhouse. "Take care no one hears you!"

"Bah! there is no one here who speaks English well enough. You must agree, John, that such meek acceptance of this tyranny is unbelievable. Our sturdy English yokels would not be so complacent. Vasilly says you must take a stick to a Greek to make him work but really there is little enough incentive for him if he is not to reap some reward for himself."

"*Signor* Nicolo was contented enough," remarked Hobhouse.

"In Iannina, yes! The business men and the merchants no doubt do very well for themselves, but these poor Greek country dwellers are another thing! Well, treat a man like a cur long enough, he will cringe like one: but the day will come when the cur will turn and bite!"

During the next few days they had opportunity enough to reflect upon the poverty of the country folk. The heavy rains had made the roads almost impassable, and the cavalcade had much ado to keep the slow and heavy horses from foundering in the mud of what in some places was little better than a track for goats. They slept in wayside hovels where the mud floors were verminous: they climbed up hills and clambered on foot down rocky precipices, leading the horses and afraid every minute that one of the beasts would slip and fall, dragging its rider with it. But the grandeur of this wild and rugged country made up for everything: and at the bottom lay their goal for the night, the town of Delvinaki – not a village of huts and hovels but a town, whose cleanly cottages beckoned a welcome.

Hobhouse slipped and cursed: Byron laughed: the Secretary twittered: Fletcher muttered: Vasilly broke into a wild burst of song: the priest blessed himself: the servants shouted: horses neighed, harness jangled: and with enough noise to give warning of an entire army they entered the little town and the Pasha's house, which he himself had vacated a mere week ahead of them.

***

It was good to change out of their dusty riding-dress and to wash away the travel stains in warm, sweet water. Supper was made ready for them with all possible speed: the inevitable chickens, eggs and grapes washed down with the local vintage, harsh and resinous.

"Do you know," remarked Hobhouse, when the first edge of appetite was dulled, "I think I shall dream tonight of beefsteak."

Byron's eyes twinkled. "Oh, coarse! coarse! When in Rome, John, you must do as the Romans and be thankful. For my part I consider this to be a fine reducing diet, if monotonous. Now, if you had mentioned partridge ..."

Hobhouse grinned. "That is to torment me, and you know it. I'm going for a walk. Will you come too?"

"Not I! I'm for my bed and as much sleep as I can crowd in before tomorrow. I'm not sure I shall be able to climb into the saddle tomorrow: I'm as stiff as a board. Goodnight!"

So Hobhouse wandered alone through the gathering dusk, along the main street and then along the green lane that ran behind the houses. The last rays of sunlight lingered on the wooded heights and he had the path to himself apart from the goats which wandered freely in and out of the vineyards, now stripped of their harvest. He found a spot to sit on a stone beside the path and listened to the silence, broken only by the tinkle of the goatbells and the gurgle of a little rivulet running over its pebbly bed. In this utter peace it was hard to believe in the realities of extortion and oppression. He watched the sun dip behind the hilltop with a final burst of fire: then sighed and shook himself. The night was growing chilly: it was time to follow Byron's example.

Their way next day led them down yet another steep and stony path and through wilder, wooded country: then, having negotiated a rickety bridge across a brawling river with much yelling and pushing of man and beast they came to a cultivated plain, divided into fields, dotted with neat villages. The contrast was startling: they might almost have been in another land and so, perhaps, they were – in Albania proper. Even the people were different. Greeks and Albanians alike wore a kind of cotton kilt, so it was hard to tell at first glance to which nation they belonged. The crops were different, too, and more varied: Byron was intrigued by fields whose lush green leaves were strange to him and which turned out to be tobacco plants. This he learned from one of a small party of Turkish horsemen who came up with them and elected without ceremony to join them on their way. The Secretary made no demur: this was a common freemasonry of the road and in company the road seemed the shorter. In no time at all, it appeared, they reached the town of

Libavako. They were still not swift enough to overtake the Pasha. The Secretary made for a house belonging to Ali's relation by marriage, who received them with as much courtesy as if he had been the Pasha himself.

"My house is honoured: pray you, enter and eat." He bowed low, hands outspread. "You cannot descend to the common lodging. The Pasha would not permit."

The Secretary interrupted the flow: the boot, he felt, should be on the other foot. "Where is the Pasha?" he demanded. "Not here? I had not thought him to be so far to the northward." He led the party in, their host coming behind, chattering all the while.

"Ali moves swiftly: not for nothing is he named the Lion! He lies in his own town of Tepellene. There you shall most assuredly find him looking for your coming. Then you shall be lodged as befits your status. For myself, my harem fills so much space I have but one poor room left for this goodly company. But I shall see to your entertainment myself. You come in a good hour: the hours of fasting are over and I shall join you myself."

"This Ramadhan imposes strict discipline," murmured Byron to Hobhouse.

"Yes: one might call it a kind of Turkish Lent: but I have noticed that these Mussulmen are good trenchermen after nightfall. Shall I lay you odds on eggs and chicken? I could eat an ox single-handed myself."

The ox was not forthcoming, but they did very well with minced mutton bound up with rice into a kind of outsize rissole, and though the chicken made its inevitable appearance it came in a highly spiced pasty served with spinach and the equally inevitable pilaff. The meal ended with fruit, nuts, sweetmeats and coffee. It was the most satisfying repast they had eaten since leaving Iannina, and though their lodging was both cramped and crowded the fare was more than palatable: which was all to the good, since renewed heavy rain kept them kicking their heels in Libavako longer than they had intended.

"You know, John," said Byron thoughtfully, watching the rain bounce off the puddles, "this expedition of ours is becoming a bore. Rain, mud and more mud: poverty, puddles and pilaff, day after day. Is it worth it?"

Hobhouse shrugged.

"It has to be. To go back would be to insult the Pasha, and from what I hear of him that would be unwise as well as discourteous."

"I believe you're right. We owe him some extraordinary politeness: and I believe we owe something too to his Secretary."

Hobhouse cocked an eyebrow. "Oh?"

"Unless I miss my guess, Fletcher wasn't so far out the other night in his fear of robbers. This is a wild country, John, and the people are desperate. We have been safe enough with the Pasha's own men to accompany us – I am not sure that I would wish to retrace my steps without them."

"Very true. We are, after all, in war territory! I understand from Vasilly that the city we see on those hills over there is the stronghold of the insurrectionist Ibrahim – that is the *petite guerre* of which the Secretary has told us that is engaging Ali's attention. It is generally believed that it will soon fall into Ali's hands, and he will then hold undisputed sway over this whole region. Indeed we don't want to upset him! *En avant*, then?"

"Needs must. Returning, in fact, would be as tedious as going on. But I wish it would stop raining."

This sentiment would be echoed by them all during the last stages of the journey. The road became more and more difficult as the mud grew steadily thicker, boiling round the horses' legs like chocolate, and the rain came down relentlessly. Both Englishmen marvelled at the chain of mountain villages, apparently hanging in mid-air: the inhabitants must be as sure-footed as the goats who wandered happily over the steep crags. It must, declared Byron, be these people who were the original Centaurs: human feet and legs could never have run free on these impossible slopes. Darkness fell early: they mistook the path and Byron, declaring that Time had forgotten its course, prepared to find himself back among the tombstones with the whole weary ride to do again. The tired horses were stumbling, in imminent danger of falling, complete with all their possessions, down the precipice: but at the first village they found to their surprise and delight that a hearty welcome awaited them. Hardly able to conceal his satisfaction, the Secretary claimed shelter for them at the home of a personal friend, a worthy gentleman whose neat and commodious abode offered them the best night's lodging they had had since leaving *Signor* Nicolo. Byron was forcibly struck yet again by the contrast between men such as this, well into Albania, and the downcast, timorous aspect of the Greek peasants.

Even the two-storeyed house held its head up, being cleanly whitewashed and with wooden flooring in place of mud. Attentive their host certainly was, but not subservient; and he expressed loud horror at the state of the travel-stained and weary gentlemen.

"Tck, tck! What a barbarous country you will think us!" he rumbled into his beard. "Believe me, it is not always this! In summer we have much sunshine, hot and brilliant: it is a pity that you should have come here in this dismal season. And then, you see, it is really very pretty, very pretty. You must seek us out again Mylord, when the sky is blue and the torrent a trickle over the rocks: and you will love it perhaps as I do. And tonight you shall sleep in a good bed with my own linen. A plague on these country blankets – fit only for horses!"

Whether it was the long hard ride or the long sleep that followed, they could not determine: but with the end in sight they were refreshed and set out to do battle once more with the highway. Battle it was: at one stage the road had been so broken by the hard rains and falling stones brought down by the wind that they had to dismount and wait while the way was cleared. A party of labourers came out from a nearby village armed with spades and pickaxes: astonishingly, all were women. Byron, exchanging glances with one black-eyed minx, could not help reflecting on some of the ladies of his acquaintance, and picturing them at such a task. Some of them, he felt sure, might be all the better for it. But no! Supposing Augusta were to be expected to wield a pick! This was no way to treat women! He had seen women in Scotland washing their clothes in the burns with stones, as indeed the village women were doing a short way away, and fetching their water in heavy pitchers, too heavy, surely, for their frail arms. But to set them to roadmaking ought to be anathema even to a Mussulman who despised all females. These villages, however, were mostly Christian: he could only suppose they had caught the infection from their Turkish neighbours.

They were now entering the final stage of their journey: despite the roughness of the road and the cheerlessness of the weather, everyone's spirits were raised at the thought, and the Albanian guides began a chanting song in which, one by one, the whole party joined lustily. They didn't know the words, but they could join in with the best. There were signs that a large town was at hand: other travellers converged on the road on horseback or in litters: and to their amazement they fell in with a heavy coach drawn by four horses. Two scruffy looking Albanian soldiers stood on the footboard: it obviously contained a person of some importance. The horses were trotting along with some difficulty and from time to time got quite stuck in the mud, whereupon anyone who was handy would be required to lend a hand if not a shoulder and give it a hearty shove. No head, however, emerged from the window to see what was happening or to thank the shovers. Byron was inclined to be indignant, but the Secretary soothed his annoyance.

"Hush! hush, my dear Mylord!" he begged. "The coach I recognise: it belongs to the Vizier! Doubtless it conveys one of the harem ladies – she must not allow her face to be seen in public, nor must we, Mylord, approach the vehicle. It would never do! It would be an insult! Dear me, yes, indeed!" And Byron subsided. He had no wish to upset that wild-eyed bodyguard.

Once across a hump-backed stone bridge, the way led them along a ledge-like path along the edge of the precipice, with the usual villages and grazing flocks on the opposite hillside. Steady nerves were needed for this, the last hazard: Fletcher's nearly betrayed him. He stopped his horse and averted his gaze. The sight of the river so far below made his head spin. "Mylord!" he cried. "Mylord!" Byron turned his head back. "What's the matter now?" he asked impatiently.

"Mylord, I cannot! I cannot do it! Oh don't ask it of me! Why did I ever leave home?"

"Oh damn you!" exclaimed Byron crossly. "You left home because you would come away: and don't say I didn't give you the chance to change your mind. Come *on*, man – you can't stand there for ever: you're blocking the way."

"Mylord, I truly cannot!"

"Of course you can! Think of King Wenceslas and tread in my footsteps. Keep your eyes on my horse's feet and follow them: don't look down if it makes you dizzy." And Byron, whose own horsemanship was not his strong point, led the way slowly and surely. He was irritated by his valet's fears: for himself he found the experience exhilarating and he drank in the stupendous view avidly. He was particularly taken with a village whose gilded minaret rose splendidly above a cypress grove: but soon there were no more villages and the road had dropped down to the river as it flowed widely but shallowly between gravel banks. The city was within sight: a thought struck him. "Vasilly!" he called. "The lady whose coach we passed along the road! It can't possibly come the way we have come – must she walk bare-faced?"

Vasilly laughed. "She will be met at the bridge, Mylord, and carried by sedan-chair on her servants' shoulders."

Hobhouse overheard and was appalled. "She must have nerves of steel!" he said. "To ride a horse was bad enough – to trust to human weakness –" Words failed him.

But Byron was laughing again. "You forget, John," he said reprovingly. "She will be veiled, and will not see the danger. There is some excuse for Fletcher, after all. But I am sorry for the servants!"

So, in the sunset glow, they came to Tepellene – and Ali Pasha.

***

That arrival in Tepellene made a tremendous impact on Byron, though the streets were dirty and ramshackle, seething with as motley a crowd as could be imagined. Albanians in long white kilts and velvet jackets, bristling with weapons: Tartars in tall caps, turbaned Turks, soldiers, slaves and sturdy citizens jostled their way along the alleys, shouting and cursing. The neighing of horses and the beat of drums added to the din: and above all rose the shrill cry of the muezzin, calling to the Faithful "La illah, illah – Llah Mohammed resool ullah!" over and over again. Their bedraggled little procession (understandably so, for they had undergone much since riding so bravely out of Iannina!) made its way straight to the Vizier's palace and through the archway in the tower into the courtyard. It was clear that here was a headquarters of war: there were soldiers everywhere and horses, ready to be mounted at a moment's notice. The very cooks who, the Englishmen were glad to see, were busy in the kitchens opening onto the court, were dressed for action with muskets across their backs. Hobhouse hoped devoutly that the call to arms would not sound before their work was finished, but had no chance to whisper this to his friend before hands grasped at their bridles and they came gratefully down from the saddle. Stiff-legged and weary, they were led up a flight of wooden stairs, along the gallery and into a large and comfortable apartment. Even here, in the gallery, there were soldiers – seated on cushions in small groups, smoking, chatting, playing at draughts. It was all very martial.

The door closed behind them. Byron thankfully sank onto a sofa in rich brocade; and Fletcher knelt to remove two pairs of muddy boots before going in search of hot water. The cushions were soft and deep. "John, I don't think I shall ever get up again," announced Byron. "How about you? I shall stay here for ever – or at least until suppertime. I could eat a whole sheep, I think. They were roasting some in the courtyard – did you see?"

Before Hobhouse could answer. The door opened again and with a sense of deja vu he saw the Secretary come tripping across in a high state of satisfaction and importance. "Ah, Mylord, I see you waste no time in making yourself comfortable. That is right and proper – it is as the Pasha wishes! His Highness asks me to convey his greetings and his assurance that your wants shall be his command while you honour his roof."

"His Highness is most kind," responded Byron gravely. "We are most appreciative of all his attentions to us."

"Of course! Do I not know it? Well, but further – he much regrets that Ramadhan" ("The Turkish Lent!" whispered Byron under his breath at Hobhouse, who frowned reprovingly) "prevents him from joining you for dinner. But be assured you shall want for nothing!"

"We are overwhelmed by this courtesy. Now, sir, you and we do not stand on ceremony with each other – we have become old friends these last days." The Secretary simpered, and looked flattered. "Pray you, sit here with us and tell us how we shall fare with the Pasha. Of what like shall we find him?"

The Secretary sat down heavily and frowned. "That is a difficult question, Mylord," he said. "Ali Pasha is – Ali Pasha! He makes his headquarters here in Tepellene because here he first saw the light: and he learned his trade in a hard school. He has seen murder and rapine dispossess his family, and he has fought his way back with strength and cunning until he is as you see him now, all-powerful in Albania. He has, of course, the full confidence of the Sultan: he is much beloved by his own people."

This was a startling commendation. "But what of those we have seen along the way who have complained of oppression and extortion?"

The Secretary was shocked – and alarmed. "Hush, Mylord! You must not say so here! Those who have made complaint have been Greek – lazy and worthless. Truly has the Pasha said of them that brother will rob brother under the very branches of the tree where the thief stands: that if a man be burned alive the son will steal his ashes to sell them." Byron's eye met Hobhouse's across the room: both were remembering, he knew, the quartered body dispersed across Iannina.

"There are strong measures," he said slowly. "Do you call them necessary?"

The little man nodded vigorously. "Mylord," he said earnestly, "a wild and sullen people needs a strong hand on the rein – in Ali's they have that hand, and they respect him: as will you."

And so it was. At noon next day, an officer whose white wand proclaimed his office, presented himself to conduct them into the Presence. The two were amused and surprised to see that the dapper little Secretary had wrapped himself for this audience in a worn and threadbare cloak, shiny at the seams, which had long since seen better days. Byron twitted him upon this, asking if his baggage had fallen unknown down the precipice. The Secretary put an urgent finger to his lips. "Hush, Mylord, hush! I do not wear my old cloak out of necessity or disrespect – I wear it as an act of policy! Yes indeed! It would never do for His Highness to think me a rich man: wars are expensive, Mylord, and soldiers must be paid! You understand? Exactly so! hush – we arrive!"

Arrive they had: the usher bowed them into a large apartment, with a marble fountain playing in the middle. As they entered, an elderly man rose to greet them – the greatest of compliments. Short, fat and white-headed, he gave an impression of power and tremendous authority: his keen blue eyes seemed to weigh them up in one all-embracing glance. His clothes were not splendid: but one touch of luxury he had allowed himself in the fine gold muslin of his turban, and his dagger hilt was studded with winking stones. He and Byron took to each other at once, and with Mylord seated at his right hand, engaged in earnest conversation with the Pasha's physician acting as interpreter. The Pasha started the ball rolling.

"You are full young, Mylord, to leave your native land and come so far abroad. Why did you do it – of necessity? or by inclination?" He seemed suspicious of his lordship's motives.

"Why, Your Highness, my friend and I had heard much of your exploits and wished to meet so great a man for ourselves, if opportunity arose," Byron answered without a blush.

"Aye!" cried Ali. "Did you then hear of me in England?"

"Naturally," Byron assured him brazenly. "Your deeds are most widely extolled in our country – isn't it so, John?"

Hobhouse looked down his nose and nodded: Ali beamed.

"Aye, so I believe. It must be so! I hear, Mylord, that you come of a great family: but that I must have known without telling, by your so small ears and hands, and by your curling hair, not lank as a man of low degree would have it."

If Ali was not impervious to compliment, neither was Byron, and the two continued to exchange fulsome compliments in a way that, as he told Byron later, made Hobhouse feel extremely unwell.

"The way you buttered that old ruffian up was almost as bad as the way he flattered you!" he told him roundly. "Have you *no* shame, you – you flaunting lordling?"

Byron's eye flashed: then he laughed. "Really? But see how well we are entertained for it!" he answered. "We have delicacies rained upon us and all that we could wish for in the way of comforts – and comfits!" he added, popping yet another sugared almond into his mouth. "Take them out of my sight, John – I shall grow fat, and that would never do."

"That's all very well, but to fawn on the old brigand the way you do is really not at all becoming."

"I don't fawn: we exchange courtesies, that's all. Besides, I'm not sure that 'old brigand' is fair."

"You know he is: you were protesting all the way from Iannina about the condition of the people and his tyranny over them."

"I know, I know – I think – no – I don't know *what* to think! I hate to see Greece under a savage heel: yet it is true enough that any people need a strong ruler and *that* the Greeks seem not to have for themselves. They are all talk and grumble: but we have seen for ourselves how ineffectual they are when action is needed. Vasilly says they need the stick: Ali applies the goad and a tight rein at the same time. I must admire him for his courage and the control he exercises – yes, and because he is not afraid to act the strong man, even though he may not be quite as famous as we have led him to believe."

"I like the 'we'!" Hobhouse flung at him.

"As I have then! I shall put him in my poem, which is coming along well. Don't let's quarrel, John! Admit that we are enjoying a tremendous adventure! Besides, in this untamed land we are better off with Ali's friendship than with his enmity."

Hobhouse had to agree: and was grateful, at their final audience with the Pasha, to receive the benefit of his advice and assistance. As they sat with him, applauding the complex gymnastics of the Court Fool, Ali turned his head and said, "Mylord, we much appreciated the honour of this visit: tomorrow you leave us. What road do you take?"

"Why, Highness, the way we came, barring flood or earthquake! And then we purpose to travel across Greece to Athens – our ultimate goal."

The Pasha's brows drew together. "Hmm! That is not good: the roads are infested with bandits who are a continual thorn in our flesh. I will give orders to the military posts along the way and they will send guards for escort. Or – even better – you may take ship at Previsa to carry you down as far as Patras. The Governor shall make arrangements and I will send also to my son Veli, who is Pasha of the Morea, that he may serve you as you may require." He smiled with satisfaction. "How does that suit you?"

"Most admirably! We are truly grateful for such consideration. May I ask one further favour?"

"Ask. If it is in my power, you shall have it."

"Will you permit us to take Vasilly with us?"

Ali looked thoughtful, then nodded. "Where is Vasilly?" he demanded. "Let him appear before us!"

"He is here, Highness, at the door."

"Then let him enter! Vasilly, Vasilly, how is it that you were without the door and did not come to see me? You know, I should have been glad to have seen you! Now listen to me, my friend: you are to return the way you came with my honoured guests: and you will see that no harm befalls them or, by the name of the Prophet, I will cut off your head!"

This last startled his honoured guests, for they realised from the sudden savagery or his tone that Ali really meant it: but Vasilly, with an unmoved countenance, merely said:

"Be very sure, your Highness: all will go well."

***

Go well it did. The storms had passed away, giving way to cloudless blue skies and milder temperatures, though a chill in the air at dawn and dusk gave warning of the approaching winter. The miry ways dried in the hot sun, and the journey back was made in half the time. Four days' travelling from Ali's headquarters saw them once more, to his great delight, safely under Nicolo's roof, and Vasilly's head was still on his shoulders.

They spent a happy, restful week in Iannina, while preparations went forward for their voyage. Sailing on the lake, riding through the countryside where all the harvest had now been gathered and next season's ploughing begun, visiting or being visited by the upper strata of townsfolk, they passed the time much, as Byron ruefully observed, as they would have done at home. Then, at the beginning of November, with a mixture of regret and anticipation, it was time to go. The advice to go by water seemed good, for reports showed that bandits were highly active round about. So they sought out the Governor who, true to Ali's order, had prepared a stout vessel for them.

Byron, early in the morning, wandered down to the quayside to watch. Their vessel was a three-masted one, long and narrow in her shape and equipped, he was glad to note, with her own armoury of cannon. Nearly all the crew were Turkish, and not many seemed, even to Mylord's inexperienced eye, to have much idea of what they were doing. There was a great deal of running about, and shouting, and cursing, and countermanding of orders: and there seemed to be a superfluity of senior officers aboard, each one reluctant to do anything really useful. Vasilly was supervising the embarkation of the baggage, and gave it as his opinion that the Captain did not know his business.

Hobhouse, who by now had come down to the jetty, looked perturbed: but Byron was unmoved.

"Which one is the Captain? For I'm damned if I can pick out anyone with authority in this lot."

"That one, Mylord," answered Vasilly with a snort, "who sits with his pipe and plays with a string of beads like a little child. Well! if harm comes to you on this voyage I shall not fear beheading, for I shall most assuredly be drowned."

Byron laughed, and clapped him on the shoulder. "Then let us drown together," he cried, and led the way on board. To his great amazement, the ship was ready to sail by noon. The anchor was raised, the wind caught the huge lateen sails, and to much cheering from the ragged urchins who throng every harbour the galliot headed out towards the bar. It was a beautiful day, with white cottonwool clouds drifting idly in the bluest of skies: the following gulls screeched raucously: the ship rose and fell gently to the sea's rhythm, and Byron, standing in the stern to watch the land recede would have been jerked nearly off his feet by a jolt that halted the vessel, had he not snatched instinctively at the rail to save himself. They had run aground.

There followed the most tremendous commotion: scurrying feet, shouts, curses, prayers and weeping. The Captain sauntered by, his face composed, still playing with his beads. Byron grabbed him by the elbow.

"What's happened, hey? What's the matter?"

The Captain shrugged, and raised his eyes to heaven.

"We have hit the land, Mylord. We are not meant to leave this day. It is the will of Heaven."

"Nonsense, you old humbug! Shipwrecked before we leave harbour? How long will it be before we can get off again?"

"Tomorrow, Mylord, if heaven wills."

"Never mind heaven! We will leave today, because *I* will it! Go and do something about it. One good push should do it."

The Captain looked resigned, and went. Hobhouse chuckled. "Very lordly, upon my word!" he teased.

"John, if you don't stop that I'll throw you overboard! As I've so often said to you, it comes in very useful at times. How long do you think it will take that lazy rascal to get us off?"

"Oh, tomorrow, no doubt – as he said!"

But it was only an hour later that the galliot finally left the shallows, assisted by the tide and a strong wind that seemed to get up out of nowhere. Then a fresh difficulty presented itself. During the afternoon the wind blew stronger and more strongly, and the gentle swell increased steadily until the ship, stout though she was, pitched and tossed. Byron was not particularly bothered by the worsening of the weather, but Hobhouse had fallen strangely silent and Fletcher, never a brave man, and convinced that he would never see his home again, called his wife's name repeatedly, to Byron's intense exasperation. Darkness was setting in: the wind was blowing still more strongly, and the helmsman, who appeared to have great difficulty in telling his right from his left, steered a course so erratic that the vessel headed straight and sure for the promontory, now no great distance away. The crew, inexperienced to a man, seeing the promontory straight ahead of them, seemed incapable of taking any kind of avoiding action until the Captain, stirred by fear from his lethargy, roared at them like any British boatswain to tack, damn them, tack or be forced to put in to a port held by the enemy French! Exhausted by this uncharacteristic outburst, he reverted to type, wrung his hands, and burst into tears: while the unfortunate crew, calling loudly on the name of Allah, wrestled with the rigging. A louder crash sounded: looking up, Byron saw the mainyard crack in two, and the foresail split from top to bottom. Fletcher whimpered, and hid his face in his hands, as the cannon, breaking loose from their lashings, rolled across the deck. The ship sat dumpily in the water, held broadside on by a steersman who had apparently lost all pretence of seamanship. Byron, raising his voice above the noise of wind and weeping, cried, "Bring her round man! Bring her round, or we shall be swamped! Good God, can *nothing* be done?"

"Nothing!" mourned the Captain, at his side.

Byron turned on him. "Can you get back to the mainland?"

"If God chooses, Mylord."

"Can you get to Corfu?"

"If God chooses, Mylord."

"In that case, *I* will choose! You have four Greeks aboard who seem to have *some* idea of manning a ship – will you let *them* handle her?"

"I will let anybody do anything, Mylord, if only we can be saved!" Whereupon the wretched man burst into a fresh torrent of weeping and fled below, crying, "Let every man put his trust in God! May Allah be merciful to us!"

Only too anxious to show their ability, and even more anxious to avoid disaster, the Greek sailors set about their task. Between them they managed to rig a couple of small staysails and to take down the huge mainsail which was taking the full force of the wind. Byron felt he could do no more: he turned his attention to his swooning valet, who clasped his hand frantically.

"Mylord, Mylord, why did we ever come?" he cried. "To think all this while we could have been snug at Newstead and not at the mercy of pirates and bandits! Why ever did we come?"

Byron grinned in the darkness, hearing the Spartan pile of Newstead being called "snug" – Fletcher used to have a different word for it! – but found it hard to curb his impatience. "Come, Fletcher, where's your spunk?" he demanded. "Remember, you *would* come, and begged me to keep you with me! Well! We set off to find adventure and here we have it. Don't repine!"

"I find I am not so fond of adventure as I thought I would be," was the unanswerable reply. "But sir, I did not think to find a watery grave."

"Since a grave is our ultimate end, I cannot see that it matters if it be wet or dry," was all the comfort he received. "I see there is no more to be said to you, and I shall try for some sleep."

Sleep he did, on the deckboards, wrapped in a huge Albanian capote: and woke to find that sometime during the night the ship had found a haven and was anchored once more close to the mainland. The complacent Turks were sitting around the deck, smoking: the Captain emerged from his refuge below decks, and to Byron's wry amusement they fell to embracing each other and congratulating themselves on their bravery in the face of extreme danger and their skill in avoiding the worst. And Ramadhan was at an end. Allah was merciful.

"We have avoided the tragedy: let us enjoy the farce," said his lordship. "What now, John? Are we marooned – or do we voyage on?"

Hobhouse, his sickness passed now that the ship was stationary once more, looked at his friend with wonder. "George, you amaze me!" he said. "I confess I have much sympathy with Fletcher, and never thought to see my home again. Yet here you have been sleeping like a baby! It passes my comprehension."

Byron looked at him quizzically. "My time has not yet come," he said. "In four or five years I might worry: in fifteen I shall be wary."

"What *do* you mean?"

"My mother was warned in a prophecy that her son would be born a cripple – and should fear his twenty-seventh year: his thirty-seventh even more. I'm too young to die – yet."

"You can't believe such stuff!"

"Can't I? I don't know: I only know that the lady was right about my beginnings – she may well be right about my end."

He thrust his lame foot out and eyed it with loathing. Hobhouse was silent – he didn't know what to say. Byron saved him the trouble of answering by saying, "Meanwhile – what comes next?"

He was answered by a shout from the shore, where a group of armed men had emerged from the trees. "More adventures for you, Fletcher!" he murmured: but it seemed these were no bandits but friendly natives, who shouted a greeting and a question. A short colloquy ensued: then, satisfied that here were no pirates, two small boats were rowed across to take the travellers to the mainland. Fletcher was unconvinced: such a rough appearance and the number and size of their weapons made him very uneasy.

"Nonsense," was the only comfort he got from his master. "You are put off by the whiskers, and a fine brave set they are." He rubbed his own chin ruefully. "For myself, I confess I shall feel the better for a shave! Do I look as fearsome? I doubt it! John, for once I believe the Captain's advice to be good: I am for making for Prevesa by land after all: I shall not trust Turkish sailors in future."

Nor was his new-found trust misplaced, since the hairy leader not only took it upon himself to feed and house the whole party and to see them safely on their way, but absolutely refused any payment for his pains. "No, no Mylord!" he declared in shocked and reproving tones. "I wish you to love me, not to pay me!"

"The hospitality of these people," said Hobhouse, as they rode off over the hills, "never ceases to amaze me. We have been made free wherever we go of all they have – and that is precious little, when all's said and done."

"Ah, perhaps that is why," replied Byron meditatively. "When you have little, you realise its value: when you have much, you despise it."

"You are not usually so philosophical."

"Perhaps this adventure has given me time for thought."

"Adventure! We certainly have plenty of that: our friends at home will have trouble believing the half of it."

"Then we shall feel natural superiority in knowing the whole. How shall we go on from here, John? Shall we get to Athens by Christmas?

"I must not be deprived of Athens – that is the ultimate goal of this Grand Tour as far as I am concerned."

"Oh, surely! The way is not so very great, and with the guards we are promised there should be no difficulty. The Pasha's signature is a powerful passport, it seems."

So it proved to be. All along the way they were welcomed, even fêted, and on at least one occasion were transported out of their real selves into a primitive world so far removed from the artificialities of polite society that only a sharp pinch could prove this was no shared dream. They had come to a small settlement inhabited only by soldiery – nothing more than a stone barracks near the shore. On the water side there was a deep cove where they could and did wash off the dust of travel with much splashing and laughter: but the captain had warned them that the woods beyond swarmed with bandits, and that by dusk they must be safely within the stockade gates. Night fell fast at this time of the year, but there was more than enough light from the huge fires kindled around the courtyard for roasting their dinner – a whole goat, no less. Then came the entertainment – and what entertainment! – as the soldiers danced their war-dance and sang their war-songs, twirling and leaping by the light of the flames to the music of the sea as it dragged back down the pebbly shore. Even Hobhouse was roused to almost poetic fervour: Byron's eyes glowed as he drank in every barbaric moment, longing for the time when he could commit the scene to paper. Fletcher waited for the end, nervous and resigned. It seemed only fitting that their next day's ride should be made under heavily armed escort, heading steadily towards the Morea. And as they went, the scenery changed and became more Greek, more and more European, not at all like the land they were leaving behind them. Indeed, at the town of Makaea they stayed under the roof of a Greek merchant who could well have been lord of an English manor, with his lawns, terraces and thickly fleeced flocks of sheep. Only the extraordinarily high, extraordinarily thick walls which fortified the house betrayed the ever-present fear of marauders who infested the country round about: and the three newly-dug graves passed by the roadside on the next day's journey through the oak woods made everyone fall silent, apprehending danger at every turn of the path. Not until the woods were left behind and the river bank was reached could they breathe freely, and the ferry which carried them over in the gathering dusk carried them also into open and freer country.

But here at Natolico, rising from the waters of the gulf like a Levantine Venice, came a setback. The Albanian Governor did not wish to know them or have anything to do with them. In fact, said the concierge with a smirk, His Excellency did no business with foreigners. Did the lame one (Byron's eyes flashed dangerously at this and he felt himself holding on to his temper with difficulty) claim nobility? "Huh!" he spat copiously. "So did many a foreigner. His Excellency had to exercise care: thus did many an undesirable claim admittance! Hearing the sound of raised voices, the Governor himself made an appearance and demanded to know the strangers' names and business. "You have done well!" he said to his underling. "We cannot be too careful in these troubled times. Leave it now to me." He turned with a sneer to Byron and said, "Well stranger? What would you do here in Natolico? And by whose order to you claim our assistance?"

"By the order of the Pasha!" declared Byron, equally haughty. "See here his signature, and his order for board and lodging for myself, my friends and my bodyguard!"

The man positively cringed, and his lordship's ruffled feathers subsided: but they were in no way smoothed when he discovered that a silent man in the corner was in fact a Greek who had recently been nominated as English Vice-Consul. "Upon my word, John!" he exploded, "this is pretty treatment indeed! Give me Albanian hospitality any day. I will not stay here any longer than is necessary: we leave tomorrow!"

And leave tomorrow they did, sending their baggage down the gulf by punt and themselves travelling as before, on horseback along the shore to the next stop on their pilgrimage. Towards the deep water of this town had been set rows of stakes and huts on poles, so that it seemed as if the little port with its lagoon had not one shoreline, but two. From the northern marshes as they approached this illusion was less apparent than from the south, the sea side: but still Byron entered the town with a strange sense of déjà vu: the marsh, the huts, the double foreshore. Missolonghi.

***

Missolonghi lay in the marshland. It was a neat little town, with tidy shops and pavements and a thriving fishing industry: but it lay in the marshland, on the edge of a vast lagoon. It was notorious for rheumatism and ague, and Byron caught a cold. He sneezed incessantly, his head ached and his eyeballs seemed to be on fire. Fletcher attended him, efficiently and mournfully.

"This is unhealthy country, Mylord," he said severely. "The sooner you are away from it the better."

"I believe you – tshoo! – are right!" conceded Byron. "Oh God, my head! I shall not stay here in this aguish place: it doesn't suit me or – tshoo! – anybody else either. To think that my pulse quickened at the thought of staying here! Why? *I* don't know. A strange appearance from the sea in the sunset – and a notion that it was waiting for me, calling to me – for what? A cold in the head, no more! Bah! Get thee behind me – tshoo! – superstition! I shan't stay here a minute longer than I must – nor must I, if I am to see Athens by Christmas, and of that I am determined! I shall send away the Albanians – no, I shall keep one as company for Vasilly – him we cannot do without! Go and see if you can find us a boat, Fletcher – a – tshoo! – *Greek* boat! No more Turks for me!"

So Fletcher set off to hire a boat, and in due course they reached Patras with a strong wind to help them along the way. Here the English Consul-General and his relation the Imperial Consul more than made up for the bad behaviour of their colleague at Natolico – they couldn't do enough for the wanderers, who felt they had reached, if not journey's end, at least a traveller's rest. The house boasted tables and chairs for one thing – on comparing notes, Byron and Hobhouse agreed that they had almost forgotten what it was to use such conveniences, and found the sensation delightful. There was a garden full of fruit and shrubs, and indeed it seemed as if the garden had spilled over onto the hillside and spread itself right out of sight. Orange and lemon trees, olives, vines and currant bushes and shrubs or liquorice clothed the hillside, topped with an ancient Turkish fortress. This was an object of scorn to the Greek inhabitants of Patras, who declared that a new coat of whitewash was the nearest it got to being put in a state of martial readiness.

During the day, Patras proved a fascinating place, full of bustle and swarming with foreign merchants who, being exempt from native taxes, could cock a snook financially at Ali Pasha and the Turkish Government. So there was much to be seen at the port, with ships loading and landing, carrying cheeses, wines and fruits, bringing coffee, sugar and all kinds of exotic produce. But even here the fog gathered thickly after sundown, and chills and agues took their toll of the unwary who stayed out of doors.

So, with his cold still hanging about him, Byron led his little band out of Patras at the beginning of December, heading eastward to distant Athens. This was more the Greece of his dreams, the Greece he had pictured from the history books and poets he had loved in his solitary childhood. Here were the mists wreathing the land in mystery: here were the groves, the rocks, the deep blue sky and the air like wine, the glittering narrow sea: and there, one never-to-be-forgotten morning as he took a stroll along the beach, rising high and snow-capped far away in the distance across the waters of the gulf, towering above all others, were the ranges of Parnassus, the very home of divine poetry. At that moment Byron, shivering slightly from the morning air and the lingering effects of ague, felt he could die happy. Then he shook himself, laughing at such morbid fancies. Of course he had no wish to die – he would live, and live inspired by the memory of Parnassus: live, and hope to see it closer and to conquer it, to climb the heights and live to be the greatest poet of his age – or if that should be too much for the gods to grant, at least *a* poet! Away with superstition! It was time to go.

For ten whole days, the party stayed in the little town of Vostizza, wholly Greek and as far removed from the bazaars of Iannina and Tepellene as could be imagined. Even the elders, the clerks and the secretaries were Greek, and the Turkish influence was thin. "Elder" seemed a strange misnomer for the Governor, who was but a youth, and a very small youth at that. Though he tried to copy the reserved and dignified air of his Turkish counterparts, it was a hopeless effort: he was too young, too boyish and altogether too small. His very Turkish cap was nearly half as tall as he was, and the sight of it sent him off into gales of merriment. The travellers had never had so much fun with a host in all these weeks. "Come, Andrea!" one of them would call. "Come and give us a show!" and he would obligingly take off his robes and cap of office and tumble about the room and over the furniture as well as any acrobat, happy to be himself again without the need to mimic Turkish dignity that his office demanded. This was how Byron had always imagined the Greeks would be: not downcast and sullen like the Greek peasantry of Albania. His mind was in a turmoil these days: torn between admiration of Ali as a strong administrator and fearless warrior, and detestation of his oppressive and extortionate rule. But whatever good he found in the Pasha, still it came down to this: that Greece, the land of Leonidas and

Demosthenes, lay under the heel of a barbarian nation and would never again be free of the yoke – barring a miracle.

Pending the miracle, he was content to spend a day or so here in this comfortable, large house with the rich carpets and snug furnishings. The ladies of the household they never saw, during the whole of their stay: the Islamic ethic had rubbed off that much, it seemed. But the cuisine was delicious and varied, and hunting parties were got up for their entertainment in the daytime, which helped to swell the larder. One day they were tempted out after a hare with as strange a pack of hounds as could be imagined: and there were woodcocks in plenty, so that they could almost pull them out of the air. It was a far cry from mud floors and boiled eggs, and both gentlemen made the most of it.

But time was passing, and there was none to lose if they were to be in Athens for Christmas. By Byron's special desire they were not to travel by the shortest route across the Corinthian isthmus but across the mainland: not from fear that the robbers who once infested the shorter road had descendants still in wait for the unwary but to fulfil the poet's dream of seeing Delphi. His brain was on fire with the impressions it had received these last two months and more: to fire his muse still further he must visit the very home of the god of Poesy. The crowning ambition of his youth was about to be realised. So to Delphi they would go, having in their sight along the way the snow-capped peaks of Parnassus.

It took them two days to get there, after being delayed by a strong east wind. But eventually the wind changed and they could be taken across the gulf in a galley powered by oars, not sails – no Turkish sails here! And finally, after two or three stops for refreshment along the farther shore, came to land at midnight, by moonlight. This was all intensely romantic: but the reality of landing brought them down to earth with a bump, for the ramshackle "han" was nearly full already. One room only could be had, and the whole party crammed in together with a large store of onions that had arrived before them – and some time before at that. They passed a miserable night, with the stench of onions, breath and bodies making an unholy pot pourri. Byron would allow no grumbling. "It is all part of the adventure," he said sternly: but he was as glad as anyone to come out early into the clean sweet air and ride north through the corn and olives towards the mountains – and Delphi.

Every step of the way seemed familiar, holy ground: every remark made by the guide brought back some memory of myth or poetry. Byron's blood seemed to surge through his veins, and when a flock of enormous birds passed low over their heads he could not contain his excitement.

"Eagles!" he cried, with a catch in his voice. "John, look! eagles! A dozen of them, I swear. Apollo be praised, he has sent his very own birds as an omen! I *shall* be a great poet – it is very clear!"

"Eagles – pooh! Vultures, belike. Take care you do not fall and break your neck in this stony place – they will be onto you like a shot."

"Nonsense, John: I know an eagle when I see one and there were at least a dozen here. How right you are about the stones – curse you! I think we shall have to lead the horses here: the way is far too steep."

Steep it was, with the bare rock now hiding the top of Parnassus from their sight, but they managed to scramble up past the small caves and burial cavities along the way. Then, leaving the horses tethered, they clambered to the ruins above the gorge where once Apollo was worshipped: broken, flattered and awesome in their loneliness. Even Hobhouse was impressed. This was a place of strange contrasts: the dirty little town along the way with its vulgar stone fountains was anything but poetic – yet they were assured that their waters came from Cassotes, the stream which bestowed the gift of prophecy.

"Shall we drink of it, John?" asked Byron. "Shall we cup our hands and learn the future? Or shall we live on in ignorance of our fate? I wonder if I really want to know it."

"Not I, I thank you! I would wager that the only future after drinking there would be short and feverish. I would not trust it."

"No? You are always so prosaic, John, and I am very sure that you are probably right. It's a monotonous tendency you have – I should never have asked you. Well! Like poor Cassandra, I daresay we should be disbelieved, so let us go on voyaging into the unknown."

It was a place full of mysteries and contrasts. Here the ruins of Apollo's temple shared a home with the monastery of the Holy Virgin: here an ancient tomb's mournful inscription jostled a column on which some modern traveller had scratched his name for posterity to read. "And after all," said Byron charitably, "in another thousand years the one will seem as pathetic as the other, so why should we rage against it?" The night was drawing in: it was time to go.

The rest of the ride to Athens, which took several days, kept up the strange contrasts: the towns were poor, the people also, and the Islamic stamp mingled with paganism. Along the way the classical ruins were succeeded by mosque and minaret, which gave way in turn to Christian monasteries. The winter weather had set in: once more they had to battle with drenching rain and wind. On Christmas Eve they were housed worse than ever before in the semi-deserted village of Scourta: here they had to share their lodging with the cows and pigs, while they slept in the loft above. "But," as Byron remarked, "there is the best of precedents for such a billet on Christmas Eve." Fletcher thought almost with longing of the customhouse room with the onions – here they were half-suffocated not by pungent vegetables but by the smoke from the fire which, as there was no hole in the roof, billowed about the stable: they were, in the morning, covered in smut and looking like so many blackamoors. To ride in the rain up a rough and rugged mountain path seemed the strangest way imaginable to pass Christmas Day: but at last the guide cried "Effendi, Effendi – to chorio, the city!" And there was the town – in a word, Athens – distant, but clearly visible.

New heart came to the weary travellers. The road grew steadily better, the weather steadily fairer: the distant citadel was steadily clearer to their sight. They had, after all, arrived in Athens before Christmas was over, and all was well.

***

"Mylord, you are most welcome: I and my daughters had not expected to receive guests at this season, and all that we have – alas, it is little enough! – is yours."

"Madam, you are very good: I can see that I shall be tempted to prolong my stay and can only wish our arrival had not been so long delayed."

The lady blushed. "You must be hungry after so long and chilly a ride. Supper will be served in – half-an-hour? So. Till then, pray make yourselves comfortable."

The door closed behind her.

"Well!" cried Byron. "It seems that fortune favours us indeed! Truly, one never knows what to expect. Two houses at our disposal! And sure, we find ourselves in the better. Three whole rooms – a bedroom each for us, who are used to sharing a sack with pigs and peasantry! We shall be wholly spoiled. The lady shows us too much favour."

"I believe she favours herself as well," Hobhouse answered drily. "I understand she is a widow, her late husband being the English Vice-Consul, and that she ekes out her impoverished means by letting her rooms to such English visitors as she may. With three daughters to support she must be glad of the income."

"Three daughters!" cried Byron. "John, how did you come by this information? I declare, you are a spy, no less. No one ever tells *me* these things."

"I doubt they dare not. You are known to be – shall we say – susceptible."

"If that is so, my susceptibilities have suffered little enough of late. The peasant women are puddings after all, and this wretched harem system has kept any real beauties well hidden from an infidel's gaze. But since Madame Macri has a faded beauty of her own, I have high hopes of her offspring."

His hopes were not to be confounded. When they took their places at table they found themselves waited upon by three of the prettiest girls Byron had ever seen, the eldest in particular having a specially brilliant black eye and thickly curling raven hair. The sweetly pensive expression of her face he found particularly charming, and when she shyly brought him a large book, asking him to write his name in it as all their visitors did, he said with a smile as sweet as her own, "My poor name is little enough to write: wait one moment, you shall have more besides." He wrinkled his brow a moment in thought: then, taking up the pen, dashed off a quick verse.

"Fair Albion, smiling, sees her son depart,
To trace the birth and nursery of art:

Noble his object, glorious his aim,
He comes to Athens, and he – writes his name."
"There! A poor effort, but mine own – I shall hope to do better before I go." He handed back the pen: their hands touched and a delicious blush crept up into her cheeks: she dropped a quaint little curtsey and retreated hastily with her book. Hobhouse, watching sardonically, gave a snort. Byron looked up and grinned apologetically. "I know – I know! But who would have thought to find the three Graces themselves as our handmaids? I'm going to like this place even more than I expected – and you know, my hopes were always high."

The first thing that had to be done was to pay a visit to the Turkish Governor, a dignified gentleman who received them with much state: the next was to plan a visit to that ultimate goal, the Acropolis. This, they found, was not an easy matter. The occupying Turks had built their own fortress on the sacred hill and the commanding officer was a choosy caretaker. His heart had to be softened: presents of tea (a rare luxury) and sugar, for he had a sweet tooth if not a temper to match, would go far to assist this process. Otherwise the gate would be firmly shut and a deaf ear turned to any pleading. Armed with this passport, they set out for the citadel, and having paid Charon his fee, as Byron remarked, were allowed to wander at will among the ancient ruins: so strange and yet so familiar, they felt that every stone, every broken column, every fragmented statue was an old and dear friend. And at last, on the very height and summit, the crown of all those marbled ruins was the Parthenon, in all its majestic glory. They had seen other ruined temples during the journey from Patras, they had just passed so many on their climb that they might well be surfeited with fallen columns and broken arches, but the Parthenon, recognised immediately, was both a joy and a despair.

To Byron, it reflected all his torn emotions concerning Greece. Ancient and beautiful, absolute in its classical perfection, it stood and crumbled. Its conquerors had formerly completed its desecration by converting it into a mosque of the meaner sort: now that too had fallen into decay and disuse. Yet still it looked down with divine serenity upon the city. Characteristically, he attempted to dissemble his feelings in public: to Hobhouse's inadequate "Well, this is all very grand!" he replied dampingly, "Very like the Mansion House. What say you, Fletcher?" Fletcher's response was even more mundane. "Ah, Mylord," he said, "what fine chimney-pieces could be made of all this marble!"

During the next three months, never a day passed without Byron visiting the classical ruins that lay within and about Athens. There seemed to be no end to them. He was soaked in, but not sated with, poetry and architecture. Every bend of a road, every twist of a path, brought some new temple or colonnade to view, when it seemed that there could be no more. The survival of the old gods gave him hope for the future of Greece: they were broken, but not destroyed. He soaked himself in antiquity by day: and in the evening, when he returned, the latter-day Graces were waiting to feed his body as the ancient had fed his mind. All three were lovely: but it was to the eldest, Theresa, that he felt himself to be the most strongly attracted. Her grace of movement, the way she would catch her lower lip in her little white teeth when some task required particular concentration, the thick black hair coiled under her veil, drew him like a magnet. He pictured that hair unbound and flowing over her shoulders in the moonlight, and his pulses quickened. One evening it happened that she waited on him alone: Hobhouse had gone off on some expedition of his own, and her sisters were busy in the kitchen with their mother. It was only the part of a gentleman to help her. She protested vainly at this.

"Oh no, Mylord: you cannot carry the pots yourself: that is the servant's work."

"And am I not yours?"

She blushed violently and retreated a step or two: not too far. "Mylord, you must not speak so."

"Why must I not, Theresa? Let us forget all this Mylording, though I love to hear the word on your lips! We are but a man and maid, and you must surely have noticed how much I admire you. You are all grace and charm – a true daughter of the Muses whom I adore – as I adore you."

The pots lay forgotten on the table: he took her hands between his own. They trembled in his fingers like frightened birds, but she did not draw them away.

"Look at me, Theresa," he murmured, his voice low and thrilling. "Look at me, and tell me your feelings for me are cold!" She peeped shyly up between her long curling lashes, and he smiled. "You see, you cannot do it! Look at me, Theresa: there will be no need of words between us."

Nor were there. She lifted her head and looked straight into his glowing grey eyes: she swayed ever so little towards him and her own closed as his hands moved to her shoulders and he bent his head to kiss her trembling lips. The door opened behind them: Hobhouse stood on the threshold as they sprang apart. Theresa gasped: snatching up his lordship's empty plate she scuttled past Hobhouse with bent head, blushing richly from neck to brow, "Upon my word, George!" Hobhouse exploded as the door closed behind her. "This is a pretty way to treat our kind hostess!"

"But I do not treat our hostess thus!" answered his friend provocatively.

"You know very well what I mean!"

"Yes: and I assure you that you are quite wrong in what you are thinking."

"To take advantage of an innocent girl under her mother's roof!"

"I have not taken advantage of her under any roof – nor do I intend to do so."

Hobhouse sat down heavily. "Then why behave as you did? This is to play with fire: take care you do not burn yourself!"

Byron's face flushed. "I am very well able to take care of myself: and of Theresa too, if necessary. She's very pretty, after all."

"That's no excuse, and you know it."

"I know it, and I cannot help it. If I promise you she will come to no harm at my hands, will that satisfy you?"

"I suppose it must."

"Then shake hands, and be friends."

Shake hands they did, but things were never quite the same between them again. Nor were things quite the same between Byron and Theresa. Hers would be the face that looked for him when he returned from the expeditions which took him further and further afield: to her he would recount his adventures as they strolled together in the courtyard under the lemon trees. When he came back from one particularly hazardous excursion, she gasped and clutched his arm: there could be only one response to that, and he promptly made it.

"Zoë mou, my life!" he murmured. "There is no call for alarm! I'm here in one piece, am I not? Though for one moment I will confess I doubted the outcome."

Well he might have done. He had gone to view the scene of the battle of Marathon, when one of his two Albanian attendants had let out a warning shout: scrambling towards them over the cliffs was a party of bewhiskered brigands, some two dozen all told, heavily armed and waving their sabres. These were no other than the notorious Mainotes, pirates to a man, who preyed on passing travellers and were not averse to capturing them for ransom if the mood took them. Byron felt completely nonplussed: there seemed to be no way of escape. Yet at sight of the scowling Vasilly the leading brigand stopped, lowered his sabre and waved back the rest of the company to a little distance. Here they held a brief conference, still keeping their eyes on the little party, and then for some reason disappeared whence they came.

"I can only suppose," Byron told Theresa, "that they imagined I had more Albanians at my back: and I saw no reason to enlighten them."

Theresa shivered. "You might have been killed," she whispered.

"But I was not killed, dear heart: I'm very much alive, as I can prove to you like this – and this!"

The days of Byron's stay in Athens passed as if in a dream, at once too quickly and as if time had been suspended. The weather was hot and sultry, too sultry: the clouds hung still and heavy over the mountaintops, waiting for they knew not what, until one peaceful evening when, unusually, the two sat together in the little sitting-room. Both were writing busily: Byron wrestling with poetic inspiration and Hobhouse, more prosaically, writing up his journal. Quite suddenly in the stillness there came a strange rushing noise and a cracking as the branches of the lemon trees shivered and broke. The door swung open of its own volition, the floor shook under their feet, and Fletcher appeared, calling urgently, "Mylord! Sir! Come out quickly, before the whole house falls! Oh, why did we ever leave home?" But before Byron could rise to his feet the shaking had stopped, the house had settled quietly into stillness, and a cooler air came through the open doorway. They waited breathlessly, but all was calm. No further tremor succeeded the first one. "You can go to bed now, Fletcher," said his lordship. "That will be all!" He chuckled. "Our Greek experience becomes more complete!" he said. "What Minos suffered, so can we!" He spoke more truly than he knew: the houses of Crete had not survived as well as the home of his Athenian Graces.

The idyll could not last. They had spent nearly three whole months in Athens: it was time to move on. Byron said a tender farewell to Theresa but his heart was not broken. Nor, he hoped, was hers. Now was the time to go, before too much damage was done.

"Goodbye, my Grace," he whispered. "I shall come back to Athens before long – will you remember me?"

"How could I forget?" she answered, shyly putting a hand to his cheek. "Forget my own Greek god – my Apollo!"

He jerked back his head. "Apollo!" he exclaimed harshly. "Apollo! Hephaestos would be nearer the mark," and he gripped her shoulders fiercely. "Isn't it? Isn't it?"

She shook her head, meeting his gaze squarely. "You take that to heart too much," she said softly. "What does a crippled body matter when the soul is sublime?"

He laughed then, and clasped her more tightly. "Ah, you pay me too great a compliment!" he said. "I do not claim to be sublime – only to follow Apollo as best I may."

"You will be great," she said solemnly. "I know it – I feel it – here!" laying her hand upon her breast. "You are putting Greece into your noble poem, are you not? I have seen you working away far into the night and I know that you will be renowned. Will you find room for me in your poem, I wonder?"

"You shall have one of your very own," he promised.

"And you will not forget me?"

"Never! I will keep you always in my heart – so you see, you must give it back to me so I may put you there for ever."

She understood what he was saying to her: she said bravely,

"Oh, Mylord, I cannot give back what I never had, but I will return that which was lent."

And so it was with head held high and a dry eye that she waved him away on the last stage of his pilgrimage.

***

Perhaps their departure from Athens would not have been so sudden had they not received a surprise visit from the captain of an English sloop bound for Smyrna who offered them a passage. It was too good an offer to miss: even Fletcher could have no qualms aboard an English man-o'-war. Both were sad to go for different reasons, but this departure seemed to have been ordained and it was with a mixture of regret and eagerness that they rode out through the gateway to Piraeus.

Arrived at Smyrna, they were given a hearty welcome by the Consul-General, so hearty that they stayed there quite happily for a full month, apart from an obligatory visit to Ephesus which swallowed three whole days. This proved to be something of a disappointment. Every relic pertaining to Artemis-worship had gone and there was precious little else to see, apart from the famed grotto where the Seven slept on Mount Prion. The few marble columns attributed to the Prison of St. Paul bore some semblance to a temple: but it was all very unconvincing, and Byron declared that a marble church seemed to be none the worse for its conversion into a mosque. The greatest excitement on this excursion was that raised by themselves when they undressed for bed, to the astonishment of the Turks who accompanied them and for whom a twice-yearly change of raiment sufficed. So all in all they were content to wander about the narrow streets of the Bazaar and to wonder at the strange humped beasts of burden which came along by the hundred, laden with goods. Sometimes the camels elected to stop for a rest and would subside, grumbling, in the middle of the road. "Just like Fletcher!" remarked Byron, cursing them with the best. Here their social life took an amazing turn for the better. Taverns abounded, and billiard rooms where two gentlemen could while away an afternoon: there were libraries where European newspapers could be had (except English ones, but they had been cut off from England for so long that they hardly

felt the loss): and balls and Assemblies to which the distinguished foreigners were more than welcome. And it was pleas-
ant enough to sit in the Consul's garden sipping sherbet, and
watching the chameleons darting in and out of the cracks in the
old stone walls. Byron was content to sit and laze and polish the
first two cantos of his poem, now complete. He read it to Hobhouse one velvet morning to the distant honking of the cranes
who flew in wedged formation northward. The effect was disap-
pointing. He had poured out his emotions, hot from his heart, in
a way that had astonished him even as he wrote: and now here
was John declaring his verses to be unworthy of him.

"No, really!" he expostulated. "Is it really so bad?"

"I did not say so: you know I am not great judge of these
things! I only say I find your sentiments exaggerated and there
is to my way of thinking a tendency to rhodomontade. You
should seek for restraint."

Byron was exasperated. "Then I'll go no further," he declared.
"Maybe they were right after all, and I shall never be a poet! I
must seek some other laurels. Shall I turn soldier? There is
much scope in this world which is constantly at war. No – there
is no room for a cripple on a battlefield. I am useless, it seems."

Hobhouse was alarmed. "Now George, I never said that!" he
cried. "Merely, you are not yet ready to rival Pope! Come, have
another glass and we'll drink to your future fame."

Byron was mollified for the moment, but that night he stowed
his poem away in the bottom of his trunk and thought no more
about it. He was becoming disenchanted with Hobhouse: they
had lived too long in each other's pockets and here, it seemed,
was proof of their fundamental incompatibility. They had been
nearly a year travelling about together: Hobhouse talked of
returning home by September while Byron intended to extend
his travels. The parting would be amiable enough, but with as
little regret as rancour.

However, they embarked together in the frigate *Salsette*,
which was going to Constantinople, to bring home the English
Ambassador. The voyage was surprisingly long for so short a
distance: quite long enough for them to make pilgrimage to
Troy – or not Troy, as Hobhouse was sceptical on that point. But
Byron's heart swelled as he surveyed the bleak and mournful

plain. No city remained, nor any stone to show that once the topless towers of Ilium had soared towards Mount Ida: only the humps and bumps of barrows that contained, so it was said, the heroes of a war fought – for love, thought Byron. Oh, love love! what havoc you wreak. How are you miscalled the gentle passion! And what has become of you, you heroes? What is there for you beyond life, that it was worth the losing? A voice called sharply, recalling him from the past to the present and the need to come aboard.

When the Dardanelles came in sight, the melancholic mood passed. Here was a challenge not only to love but to youth indeed, and he determined that, strong and enthusiastic swimmer as he was, the Hellespont he must and would cross as once Leander did but with, he hoped, greater success, although no Hero waited on the other side. On investigation he discovered that the customary passage followed Leander's route, which took advantage of the current but meant a four mile swim in either direction, though as a fish swam the distance was no more than a mile at most: and "I doubt," he said, "whether Leander's conjugal affection must not have been a little chilled in the passage to Paradise." There must be a better way. "I will race you, Mylord!" said a Mr Ekenhead who was of their company, and "Done!" cried Byron without hesitation.

So one afternoon the two set off side by side with a boat following them in case of accidents. The weather remained warm, the sky blue: but both gasped when they entered the icy water. They had not believed anything could be so cold. For an hour or more they struggled but the bitter wind and the strength of the current which was against them proved too much and they had to be hauled gasping into the boat like a pair of flatfish.

"You must give up the attempt," Hobhouse urged. "Now you see why Hero waits in vain: there is nothing left to prove."

"Nonsense," panted Byron, feeling the life flowing back into his numbed limbs, "we will pick a better time and place and try again."

Try again they did, on a warm May morning with the tide running less strongly and Hobhouse watching disapprovingly from the frigate where she rode at anchor under the castle

walls. Byron said afterwards that he had never been so exhila-
rated in his life as when he battled with the waters of the
Hellespont. His limbs seemed to receive new life as the pair of
them, swimming strongly, came down the strait and into the
bay. Even the fish seemed to enjoy it and came beside them as
if trying to determine what strange finless specimens these
were. At last his feet touched bottom: he stood up, shaking the
water from his face and saw, somewhat to his chagrin, his
companion already waiting for him on the beach. Mr Ekenhead
had beaten him by five minutes. The chagrin did not last: he
had swum the Hellespont! He took a childish, bumptious joy in
his exploit, and everyone had to hear about it.

Constantinople took them straight into the Arabian Nights.
The gorgeous palaces, the gilded domes and minarets, the
crowded bazaars, were Iannina and Tepellene all over again,
multiplied a hundredfold: and the same monotonous cry rose
over all "La illah, illah-llah Mohammed resool ullah!" But this
was Turkey itself, and where the Sultan was all this was right
and proper: even in Albania it did not seem too misplaced. It
was its manifestations in Athens that irked the western traveller: and it was in Athens that resentment had simmered beneath the surface. In his mind, Byron compared the smooth
acceptance of Nicolo with the sullen resignation of the Greek
peasant: then moved on to the scarcely-veiled loathing expressed by the Athenian citizens. There would be a reckoning
some day – he felt it in his bones.

Nevertheless, Byron was well content for the time being to
savour all that Stamboul could afford, to laze about smoking an
idle pipe, to affect to be completely blasé about the wonders that
unfolded before him. He genuinely felt St. Sophia to be altogether inferior to St. Paul's, and said so, explaining his preference
by saying, "I speak like a cockney!" Half of him was absorbed by
the wonders of the East and half of him was sated with new
impressions, and since Stamboul made him free of all she could
afford, this seemed less than grateful. They were taken, as
honoured guests, to view the dancing dervishes, and came away
dizzy and bewildered: they were entertained at the Seraglio and
received by the Sultan in person, and the chief impression was
of darkness, gloom and a heavy feeling of oppression.

He would have idled away the months in a contented dream, had it not been for Fletcher's constant repining, and it exasperated him. "The trouble with you," he informed his valet tartly, "is that you are far too nice in your habits! You despise the foreigner and all his works – pray you, remember that in his country *you* are the foreigner! You long for good, sensible beef and beer – in *this* climate? You cannot eat pilaff? But I can – and if I can, so can you! You cannot drink strange wines? Then you deprive yourself most wilfully. You have to sleep in strange beds or no bed? And so, my friend, do I! You put me out of all patience with you! Let me hear no more of it!"

Startled into silence, Fletcher kept his resentment to himself, but all these pinpricks were adding up in Byron's mind and when Hobhouse announced his intention of returning home with the ambassador, he announced that he was coming too.

Hobhouse was surprised.

"I thought you were determined not to return home for some time yet?" he remarked.

"I'm not going to. But I've had enough of these Turks. The Greeks will, sooner or later, rise against them: it is already more than time. I shall come with you a part of the way only, and pass my summer among my friends the Greeks of the Morea."

"What of Fletcher? He is no friend to foreign travel. Shall I take him along with me?"

Byron smiled suddenly. "No indeed! Would you believe it, he has petitioned me to take him with me and I have said I will take him, although I had to speak sharply to him the other day. I'm glad of it: I don't really know how I would go one without him! He is, I suppose, very patient with me despite his grumblings."

So it was arranged. The short voyage blew away much of Byron's ill-temper, and when the final parting came it was with amity and good humour. With only his two Albanians and Fletcher for retinue he felt, so he said, like a modern Robinson Crusoe, left to fend for himself among strangers.

"You'll do very well, I daresay," said Hobhouse drily.

His lordship smiled. "Well! We shall see. Do not go without some remembrance of me." He turned, and picked a handful of flowers, growing wild along the shore. "We will each keep half to take on our separate journeys to remind us of our travels together, shared like this poor nosegay."

Hobhouse took his half with a smile. "I will keep it," he promised, "until it withers." And so they parted.

Left to himself, Byron headed for Athens and his present mood seemed changed. Even Theresa was changed, and he realized with relief mingled with pique that he could no longer move her. She was armoured against him.

"Have you forgotten me so soon?" he reproached her.

"No, Mylord. I have not forgotten – anything. I remember every word you ever said to me."

"I said I held you in my heart."

"True: and that heart you asked me to return."

"Will you receive it again?"

"No, Mylord: I want no second-hand goods from you or anyone."

Stung, he turned to drama. Taking his Turkish knife from his pocket, he cried, "Then I will stab myself! See! here in that heart which holds you: and so I stab you too!"

She smiled. "I thank you for the compliment," she said. "So large a heart must hold a goodly company – I shall not die alone!" She turned away: he could make no impression on her.

It was with relief that he turned his face northward to pass the summer, as he intended, in the Morea. He had found Patras delightful on his first visit: he found it no less so on his second. He was happy to travel about and to visit the son of his old acquaintance the Pasha: even more delighted with the splendid horse he received from him as a present. But along with remembered delights went remembered distempers. On his first visit he had caught a cold, so he was not altogether surprised when one day he started to sneeze. He tried to ignore it, but by evening he was shivering violently and glad to retire to bed. To bed, but not to rest, for his head ached abominably and so did all his limbs and joints. By morning, he was tossing in a high fever; and Fletcher, alarmed, sent for the English consul.

"It is the Morea fever," this worthy pronounced. "It comes blown on the wind from the marshland. We are inured to the miasma – strangers are, ah, highly susceptible, especially when delicately nurtured."

"What is to be done?" asked Fletcher fearfully.

"There is little that can be done," answered the other. "The fever either burns itself out – or not."

"A doctor! A doctor! We must fetch a doctor at once! At once do you hear me? At once!"

"Yes, yes, I hear you," the consul said testily. "The whole town can hear you, I have no doubt."

"Then fetch one immediately! Mylord must have the best attention possible – *I* do not know what to do for the best."

The consul looked at the patient, who was muttering incoherently.

"We can do better than that – we can fetch two."

"Then hurry, hurry!"

The consul looked at Fletcher with dislike – he objected to this urgency from an underling. Nevertheless, as the case indeed appeared desperate, he sent his servant to fetch the two physicians who lived in Patras. Both gentlemen were most luckily at home and before long were bending with much solicitude over their noble patient.

"Go away!" groaned the sufferer. "Go away! Whoever you are, friends or devils, go away!"

"Mylord is delirious," pronounced the elder of the two. "He must be blooded immediately to reduce the fever."

"No!" screamed Byron. "I've never been bled! I *won't* be bled! Go away!"

The two Albanians, who had remained impassive the while, looked threateningly at the medical men. "If Mylord dies," said one, fiercely, "you too shall die," and the other, hand on the hilt of his dagger, nodded agreement.

The doctor drew himself up, much aggrieved. "He will not die if you will do as I say," he remarked coldly. "If he will not be bled, he must be purged. We will administer an emetic – we will apply a clyster. The whole system must be cleansed. Here, you! hold this basin, and you!" – to the second man – "support Mylord as I shall show you. This one" – indicating the indignant Fletcher – "will be of little help."

It was a short illness, but severe. Mylord lay and shivered, submitting to the drastic measures of his medical attendants with a very ill grace. In his weakened state he longed for death, if only to rescue him from their punitive descents upon him. The week seemed a year: but at the end of it he rose, pale and exhausted, feeling that he had survived despite their ministrations. He determined to return forthwith to Athens. Patras was obviously unhealthy for him: he remembered that the cold he had caught on his previous visit was the worst he had ever had. So, weak from his illness and very much thinner, he returned: not to the house of the Graces but to a Capucin monastery whose perfect setting had impressed itself on him on his previous visit. With Hymettus in front of his, the Parthenon behind and the Temple of Zeus on his doorstep, what more could a poet ask? There was even a library all among the orange trees: and as the good Papas were not too strict in their monastic calling he found the life entirely suited to his character. The monastery included a school for boys, and he joined joyfully in their games. He felt himself a schoolboy again, happy to take Italian lessons from one of the pupils, a French lad called Nicolo – "How that name follows me about!" he laughed – and swore he made as little progress now as he did when at Harrow. "But all knowledge is useful," he cried, "even if one has very little of it."

But still the restlessness plagued him: and other considerations decided him to move on again. Madame Macri had heard of his return and waylaid him, reproaching him on two scores: that he spurned his former lodging and her daughter together. That Theresa's heart was broken he did not at all believe, even though his conscience did prick him a little when he thought of their last parting. Her mother's ambition was a different matter: it was clear that she would marry them off if it lay in her power to do so. So persistent was she that he had to resort to playing on her naturally superstitious nature, and to relate to her that incident which dogged him from time to time and which he would thrust resolutely to the back of his mind.

"Ah, Mylord!" sighed the lady. "I had not looked for you to treat my innocent child in such a way!"

"What way is that, Madam?" he asked, with ice.

She looked a little confused at this.

"What way?" he pressed.

"Why, Mylord, to leave her alone and heartbroken. Did you not lure her with vain promises?"

"Come, Madam, let us understand one another! I never lured anyone in my life, and you know very well that there were never any promises between me and your daughter. This is but your own ambition speaking, and you know it! She would never be happy as my wife even if it were not foretold in the stars that this cannot be!"

"The stars, Mylord? *Cannot?*"

His voice sank. "The stars, Madam. You must know that before my birth my mother was assured by a soothsayer that her son would be a cripple" – his mouth twisted – "and that his – *second* – wife would – yes, be a foreign lady. So you see, your daughter must wait her turn."

"Ah, how cruel you are! and I had thought you noble!"

"Noble, yes, and – kind, Madam. If I were cruel, then I would wed Theresa. She is – and will be – happier by far without me."

She saw that it was useless and was wise enough not to pursue the matter further. But the exchange had nettled him and he informed Fletcher that it was time to move on again. He was wryly amused to find that Fletcher, who so often had bewailed his parting from his own wife, had found consolation elsewhere, and appeared resigned now to prolonged absence. "Dare you then face an expedition with me again?" he asked.

"Why, yes, Mylord," the valet answered primly. "I know what I can expect, which will not be much: and what a tale I shall have to tell my grandchildren."

"Oho! so you expect to have grandchildren? I wish I could think the same."

"It is usual, after all, Mylord."

"Yes, it is usual. But I have the strangest conviction that the usual blessings of this life will be denied me. Meanwhile, we must do the best we can, and I will go to Egypt."

But this was easier said than done. He was obliged to wait for the necessary papers, and other problems arose of a more pressing nature. For some time he had been troubled about his finances, and rather than forfeit Newstead he determined to return and save it. He had no particular desire to live in England: he had come to feel Greece and the Greeks a part of himself. But Newstead called more strongly still. He felt low and dispirited: and quite suddenly he felt the need to confide in the only person who had ever understood him or shown him any real and disinterested affection. His mother found it difficult, if not impossible, to show her emotions openly: that she was fond of him he did not doubt, but he could never forgive her for the disability that he always felt, perhaps irrationally, was all her fault. With Augusta it did not matter. He would go home to Augusta and she would laugh him out of the dumps and listen to his poetry and encourage him to believe that he was worth something after all. Damn Hobhouse! What did he know about it?

His mind once made up, he pressed ahead with his arrangements, until the day of departure was upon him. His belongings were safely stowed, with the precious manuscript still at the bottom of his portmanteau, and at last he stood on deck watching the coast of Greece recede in a sunset of rose and pearl. Before him lay poetic fame and personal notoriety: behind him, he left youth, romance and adventure. He would never be so happy again.

***

ENTR'ACTE

On a hilltop above Genoa, the Countess Teresa Guiccioli sat sewing in the pretty garden of the Casa Saluzzo. At least, her nimble fingers were busy as she sat among the orange trees: her mind was busy elsewhere, and her needle darted mechanically in and out of the fine fabric. The Countess was not happy. She felt a black cloud gathering above her head! It had been gathering for weeks, and she felt that at any moment the storm would break.

A halting footstep sounded behind her on the terrace: she turned, dropping her embroidery as she stretched out her hand with a welcoming smile. "Mio Bairon! I did not know you had returned. I thought you still in Genoa! Has your business prospered?"

He sat down beside her, a gentleman approaching middle age, slight and greying. "Yes," he said. "I have been to the bank to see Mr Barry. Everything is settled."

A cold hand clutched at her heart: the cloud settled lower over her head. "Theresa," he said, with his eyes fixed on the blue waters of the bay, "I have something to tell you."

She waited, hardly daring to breathe.

"I am leaving you for a little while."

"Where – where are you going?" she whispered.

"I am going to Greece."

The cloud burst. "To – Greece?" she uttered, disbelieving. "To Greece?" Then, springing to her feet, she cried, "In God's name, why?"

"Because she needs me."

She stared at him. "Do *I* not need you? As the breath I breathe, as the light I see? Why Greece, dear God?" her voice rose to a shriek.

He said, "It will be hard to explain, but I will try. You know that the Greek patriots have risen against their Turkish rulers.

Some call it an insurrection: I see it as a war of independence. I saw it coming, years ago. Now – it has come."

"And that has been worrying you? I knew you were worried – I asked you to share your thoughts – but you would not tell me. You shut me out. You have been cruel – cruel!"

He said patiently, "The time had not yet come. I am telling you now."

"You are telling me that which kills me! I do not see why you must go. You must not go – you will be killed – you must stay here."

"I must go because it is my fate – my *moira*. My life has fallen into a pattern. As a young man I travelled Greece for my pleasure – now I see that it was a preparation. I am called, it seems."

"You are called, indeed! What sick fancy is this?"

"No fancy, my dear. Now, you are aware that a committee has been formed in London, of noble gentlemen pledged to support the ideals of a free Greece – the companion of my former travels is one of them. Indeed, we have entertained two of them here, under this very roof."

"I remember. They talked to you long, and in secret. Ah! if I had known what they were about, I would have poisoned them!"

"Very likely. Well! I have been elected a member of that committee: and I am determined to go and see for myself how matters stand, and to do what I can to help."

"You are determined to go. Yes, you are determined to leave me – you will leave me forever – you will go – and you will never come back! Do I not know it?"

"You know nothing of the sort!" he answered. "Of course I will come back!"

"Why cannot some other of these – noble gentlemen – go? Why not the friend of your youth? Why you – when you are wanted – *needed* – here?"

"Because," he said, still patiently, "I am wanted – needed – *there*. Of them all, none knows Greece as I do, who have spent weeks and months with her people. I've slept in palaces and in pigsties, I've travelled by ship and on horseback – even on a mule – I've been up mountains and over marshes – I've known tempests and earthquakes – and I've talked with the people. By

God, I've talked with the people! This thing has been fermenting for years – now it has boiled over."

She said contemptuously, "It is not really you they want – do you know that? It is your money! Do not tell me – I know. Why do you not just send the money and let them fight their silly war for themselves?"

"Because I am a realist. Of course it is the money they need – wars are expensive! But I must be sure the money is not wasted. I must be sure that it reaches the right hands, and is used in the right way."

"So you do not trust them?"

Surprisingly, he answered, "No – I do not trust them. I sympathise with them, I will fight for them, I will even love them – but I will not trust them."

"You do not trust them! You admit it! Yet you still say you must leave me – leave your home – leave everything we have built together for them! Do you owe *me* nothing, who have sacrificed all – all for you?"

He came to her, and took both her hands in his. "I owe you – so much," he said. "But I owe something, also, to myself. You spoke just now of trust. Do you not trust me? Do you not trust me to return when my work in Greece is done? Do you not trust me to return – here – where I know you will be waiting for me? You see how I trust you!"

She broke free from his grasp. "You argue like the serpent! It makes no matter what I say – you have made up your mind to go! You do not ask – you are telling me! Is that not so?"

His jaw hardened. "As I said at the start of this argument – yes. I am telling you."

She knew from the note in his voice that his mind was, in fact, made up: she could not know how hard the decision had been. She would make one last throw – she would hit him, hard – below the belt if necessary.

"And what," she asked, "of your famous prophecy? Hasn't it been proved so far? Remember your second, foreign wife! Remember the danger of your thirty-seventh year! It is nearly here."

"I remember," he answered curtly. "I remember too, my love, that you are not, after all, my wife."

Her eyes filled. "How cruel you are!" she cried. "What else have I been to you these last four years? In the sight of God ..."

He interrupted her. "Oh, in the sight of God, my dear, I have been as polygamous as any savage for many years more: long years before ever we two met and loved and ..."

"Don't go on! Don't go on! You promised – ah, you promised you would not leave me unless I wished it ..." Her voice became wholly suspended by tears – she turned away, wrenching her handkerchief between her fingers until the thin fabric shredded.

He came behind her and turned her to face him. His hands were surprisingly gentle. So was his voice.

"What do you wish then, my dear?" he asked. "Do you wish me to betray my honour – God knows there is little enough left to me! – And stay on your silken leash? No – no – my mind is made up. I shall go to the one place where I know I can be of use: where for once I can play the man's part and redeem the wasted years. It is not often that we are given a second chance, you know: now that it is held out to me I dare not refuse: it will never happen again."

"Yes," she whispered brokenly. "You are tired of me: you are tired of me as you tired of all the others: you do not know the meaning of love."

He smiled wryly. "There are those who say I know it only too well! I love you so much that one twitch of that silken leash will bring me hasting back to you: I love you so much that I know you will not twitch it lightly." He lifted a long golden lock of hair and made as if to twine it round his throat. "See! See how you hold me as I shall hold you in my heart across the miles. I love you and will always love you, my last, last love: but you are a woman and you cannot understand that love must share a man's life with honour and duty and a thousand other things. That is your tragedy."

She sighed, and dropped her head upon his breast. "Yes, you are a man, and do not know how everything we feel, or say, or do, must be bound up with you as you are bound now with my own hair! You have been planning this for many days now, is it not? And you have made up your mind without me. Well then, go: go, my *cavaliere servente*, and be again a *cavaliere errante*, while I stay among the oranges and water them with my tears."

He drew a deep breath – of relief? The moment of acceptance had come more quickly that he had feared – and raised her head. "No," he said, "you shall not be so poor-spirited. You will go on living until my return and I shall remember you with laughter and return the quicker." He bent his head and kissed her, gently as a breath: and then harder, with insistence. "So I seal the bargain!" he said. "Come! let us make the most of the days that are left."

Those days passed in a fever of preparation: there were long sessions with Barry the banker, a ship to be chartered, stores to be collected. And always, always, Teresa. One moment she would demand to go with him: another she would cling to him as if she would never let him go to Greece or anywhere else. Everyone, she declared, was against her – even her own brother had deserted her and would sail away with Byron – she would never see either of them again in this life. If only she had been a man – then she could have gone too. Exasperated, Byron commented that had she been a man, their relationship would never have happened in the first place, whereat she left the room, pale and outraged.

Although Byron would not own it – could not, after the emotive scenes through which he had passed, that drained him of energy – his mind was in fact in a state of flux. He had talked to Teresa in grandiose terms of his honour and of a high call to action. He could not back away from that decision, nor would he be granted a second chance of making it. To tell the truth, the decision had not been made by him, but for him: made by the force of circumstance and by pressures which beset him on all sides. Teresa had spoken no less than the truth when she accused him of plotting behind her back: but in fairness to himself he maintained that the plotting was not of his making. The Greek Committee had made him one of their number: he was familiar with Greece and the Levant in general: he had claimed that this was the one country where he had ever found true contentment.

For all that he had pooh-poohed the notion, his darkly superstitious streak clung to that old prophetic foolishness: the forewarning of death could not be banished from the enterprise and he had sought to rationalise his fears by pointing out that, in all truth, the Countess Guiccioli was not Lady Byron. And what of her? He had treated her abominably whom once he had revered as the only woman he wished honourably to possess: she had gone on loving him, having borne from him more than any other woman would and having borne to him the daughter he would never see, he knew, again in this life. One moment he would be overpowered by the longing he dared not admit to see his wife and daughter, to revisit his native land: the next, he was resigned to making restitution for the past follies and vices of his life by sacrificing it in a cause about which, if he were to be honest, he was in two minds. But he had gone too far: there could be no going back now.

The day of departure dawned. The baggage was bestowed, the carriage made ready, and Byron, his final farewells said, clambered in and was driven where glory waited.

Teresa, at the end, remained calm and dry-eyed. Her emotion had been spent: she would not recriminate any more but sent her hero off to the Grecian wars like any Spartan wife. She stood where he had left her after that last, long, farewell embrace: and when the carriage was lost to view of her straining eyes then, and only then, did she turn, run up the villa's stairs and cast herself on her bed in a passion of weeping. She did not care for honour, duty or the pointing finger of a censorious world. She knew only that she loved him, would always love him – and she had lost him. Not even the last scribbled words sent to her from Leghorn could ease the ache in her heart and mind.

"My dearest Teresa,

I have but a few moments to say that we are all well – and this far on our way to the Levant. Believe that I always love you and that a thousand words could only express the same idea ...

Ever dearest yours.

NB"

***

PART TWO
THE BAYS

The brig *Hercules*, strong by name, certainly didn't look it. Edward Trelawny went so far as to call her an unseaworthy old tub: an experienced soldier of fortune, he fancied he knew all about ships and the sea. "Collier-built," he sneered. "This infant's cradle will do anything but go ahead." Mylord smiled, and ignored him. He was too busy seeing that all his party and stores were safely aboard. There was certainly enough to see to. Besides themselves were Teresa's brother, Pietro Gamba; the doctor; Prince Mavrocordato's relative, Schilizzi; and no fewer than eight servants to attend them, including the faithful Fletcher and the Italian Tita Falciere. There had been some trouble finding a doctor to go with them. An Englishman's skill Byron would have trusted, but with one eye on the coffers he felt that he could not afford such a luxury. Pietro, conscientious and willing though he was, was no help at all: he had no idea where to come across an Italian with sufficient experience for such an enterprise. His vague enquiries met with little success. Then out of the blue came a suggestion from the English doctor at Genoa, and Dr Francesco Bruno came aboard. He wasn't, at first sight, altogether a happy choice: he seemed uneasy and tended to jump out of his skin whenever Byron spoke to him.

There were two dogs, goodness knows why – a bulldog named Moretto and Lion, an enormous Newfoundland which had been given to Byron as a present and from which he refused to be parted. Then, apart from the food, there were five horses, and the military equipment and medicines necessary for a martial undertaking. Trelawny would have done it better. He said so himself.

"The Archipelago is alive with Turks and marauders – a fast-sailing vessel is essential to get us there without hindrance. In this – this *thing* – we shall be stopped before ever we get started. I wish you had left it to me to find you a decent ship."

"Never mind," was all his lordship would say. "You are come to give me aid in the enterprise, not to act as quartermaster. You know your assistance will be invaluable."

Trelawny sniffed. "Flattery," he said, "will not keep us afloat. Where do you plan to make landfall in Greece?"

Byron picked up a letter lying open before him. "The Prince's brother Constantine has advised me to base myself at Missolonghi in Aetolia. I know it well – and could have wished for other advice. The first time I went there I caught a bad cold: then I nearly died of a fever contracted there. I equate it with sneezing, shivering and a diet of toast and water. *Che sera, sera*: according to this, it is 'the one point in our dear Fatherland which is most threatened by the enemy and the weakest and most in need in present circumstances.' So. I am further advised to contact General Marco Botzaris, captain of the Souliots – that is also the opinion of the Metropolitan Ignatius in Pisa."

"Well, that's all very helpful, but is there no real news?"

"None. In fact it has been suggested that we delay our departure. I won't do it. I've put my hand to the plough, and we will sail tomorrow."

Trelawny was startled. "Tomorrow? On the *13th*?"

"Why not?"

"No reason at all, I suppose. Yet – the 13th? I'm enough of an old sailor to be superstitious, and I don't like it."

"I'm superstitious myself – perhaps that's why. I don't expect to return, you know."

Trelawny laughed uneasily. "Why ever not?"

"Next year will be my thirty-seventh. I have always known that it would be dangerous for me. It is part of an old prophecy – and all the rest has come true."

Trelawny was intrigued in spite of himself. "And what was the rest?"

"That I should be born a cripple: which I was. That my second – wife – would be a foreign lady: which in effect she was. That my twenty-seventh and thirty-seventh years would be dangerous for me."

"You survived the twenty-seventh."

"I married."

It was said flatly, without emotion, but even the hard-bitten Trelawny felt a quiver down his spine. He said carefully, "And you believe such things?"

"My mother was Scottish. I believe in the second sight, yes: though thank God, I have not the gift myself."

"Despite all this, you sail on the 13th!"

"Oh, yes – I defy fortune, you see. I shall sleep on board tonight, and we will be off in the morning, so you had better sleep here too."

So that night, as if it were a rehearsal, these strange shipmates crowded into the clumsy little brig, rocking gently at her moorings in Genoa harbour, almost lost among the taller spars of the larger vessels around her, whose lanterns cast little pools of light upon her decks. Confined below decks, it was stuffy in the extreme and no one slept more than fitfully, if at all, each alone with his thoughts. It was odd to be thrust into this intimacy with such an ill assorted company: yet had he not in his youth spent stranger nights in odder places? Everyone was glad when that interminable night came to an end and it was time to go.

Sail on the 13th they did – after a fashion, slowly beating out of harbour with what little wind there was: there was so little that for the whole of the day Genoa remained in sight. But when the moon rose, the wind rose with it and as if to make up for its previous inertia threatened to bear out Trelawny's gloomy prognostications. The ship heaved and wallowed: and most of the passengers heaved with it: Pietro lay moaning in his bunk, unable to lift his head. Byron, unaffected by the motion, remembered with a sudden brilliant clarity another ship in another storm and a young man attempting to re-lash a broken loose cannon. This time it was two unfortunate horses which broke loose, kicked down the flimsy partition which separated them, and staggering badly on the rolling deck crashed into each other before they could be caught by the head. One was badly lamed: he could only hope that fomentations would reduce the swelling that was already rapidly forming. He felt intense pity for the poor brute. "To think," he reflected, "that it was an act of mine, of all men, that brought you to this pass." He shook himself mentally – he was becoming fanciful, seeing in the laming of a horse that would undoubtedly have to be shot if the injury proved severe a reflection of himself. The captain loomed up beside him. "It is no use, your lordship: we must head back to Genoa." Byron nodded. There was nothing he could say: and twenty-four hours after the enterprise began they re-entered the port. It would take all day to make repairs: Byron decided, on an impulse, to return to the villa.

"A bad beginning," he said to Pietro, "is a favourable omen. Come with me: I would like to see my home once more."

Too late. Teresa, who had been unable to face life alone in the villa they had shared together, had already left, and the rooms were bare, deserted, hollow. Byron had arranged that Barry the banker should become his tenant during his absence, but he had not yet moved in and the villa was lonely and desolate. Wisps of straw from the packing cases blew idly across its marble floors: it was a melancholy sight and did nothing to raise Byron's spirits. "Where," he asked Pietro, "shall we be in a year?" Pietro did not answer: there was none to give.

So, instead of sitting where Teresa had first heard of his intention, Byron spent most of the day with his brother-in-law by courtesy and his prospective tenant in the public gardens, brooding over past follies and future prospects, jerking his lace-edged handkerchief between nervous fingers. It was an inauspicious start. But once fairly at sea again he found he could shake off all gloomy thoughts and look ahead with enthusiasm, even eagerness. He was actually bound again for Greece, whose memory had haunted him all through the wasted years: he felt young again and thirsty for adventure. He had made some mark with his pen, he knew, despite his tarnished reputation: now he would show the world his mettle with a sword. He was glad that there had been no second farewell from Teresa – he would write to her from Leghorn.

His spirits rose by the hour. The weather was fair, but the wind was again so slight and the sea so calm that the voyage to Leghorn took five whole days. All the while, his lordship remained on deck, aloof from his companions even at mealtimes, and sleeping under the stars. It was a quiet and peaceful life, each man keeping his thoughts to himself. Trelawny could make nothing of it: he was restless and exasperated. If only he could have had the handling of this expedition! Never mind, once in Greece he would shift for himself: he would see what was to be done and get on with it.

At Leghorn, the motley party was augmented. They were all startled as they entered the harbour to be greeted by a 15-gun salute from a vessel already moored there: poor Dr Bruno jumped quite two feet in the air, when the first salvo boomed across the water. It came from a Greek frigate under the command of one *Signor* Vitali, who, having been promised a passage to Greece with his lordship, came straight aboard, sure of his welcome. He brought with him some Greek merchants, also heading for home to join their countrymen at war, and they were full of rumours. Trelawny was horrified at the tales they had to tell: he swallowed them whole.

"Mylord, you must take every care," he urged. "Be upon your guard! I have it on excellent authority that *Signor* Vitali is in the Sultan's pay and will hand you over to the Porte as soon as may be. So much for morality of the modern Greek!"

"Aye, have you so?" asked Byron absently: he was reading a letter which had been awaiting his arrival.

Nettled, Trelawny went on, "What is more, this man Schilizzi who claims to be Prince Mavrocordato's relative – he is an imposter, an agent for the Russian Government! For God's sake, Mylord, take care of yourself!"

"Well, so I shall, and of you too, be sure."

"I thank you! I can take care of myself as well as any man," retorted Trelawny, his hawk eyes flashing. "And this man Hamilton Browne – who is he?"

"A most welcome adjunct to our party – he has seen service in the Ionian Islands and his experience will be invaluable. Do stop fussing, there's a good fellow."

"Oh, if your letters are more important than possible attempts on your life, I have done!" said Trelawny, and flung away in a temper.

The letter was very important, or so Byron thought. It contained some verses of well-wishing from no less a person than Goethe: it seemed that the luck was changing.

Almost unnoticed, the little ship quietly raised anchor and lurched her way out of Leghorn harbour, out into the Mediterranean. The quays, the warehouses fell steadily away behind her: the coast of Italy slid slowly past her to port: and as one well-known landmark after another came into view and was left behind so were all thoughts of melancholy. The monotony of these days at sea had to be broken: they fenced and boxed with each other and practised their markmanship with the unfortunate gulls as targets. "It's all good practice!" said Byron merrily: he was becoming more and more like a schoolboy on holiday. Trelawny was changing his opinion of him. He had chafed at the thought of Byron's assuming seniority over the expedition, but "Do as you like!" was his lordship's response to questions and in the end Trelawny stopped asking them. He could make the decisions: he asked no better.

His own temper varied on the edge of petulance: he became impatient with small setbacks. The discovery that the green uniform jacket, frogged and braided, that he had ordered from Vienna was too small vexed him beyond measure, and he threw it from him with an oath. Byron picked it up and examined it.

"This is very fine, upon my word. I believe it would fit me."

"I hope it does: it is no good to me. You may have it with my very good will."

"Fletcher! What have I got to land with in Greece?"

"Nothing, Mylord, but your old tartan jacket."

"Then I will land in this, and impress everyone with my martial appearance. It fits like a glove and is very apt for a General."

This incident gave him an idea. "Edward, are you game for a lark?"

"You know I am at your service."

"That's not what I asked you! This jacket of yours fits me well – but what of our gallant and gross captain's scarlet waistcoat? Do you think it would fit us both – at the same time? Shall we try?"

"How will you get hold of it?"

"When he takes his siesta. It is very hot – he will be sure to take it off."

The cabin-boy was despatched on this larcenous errand: Trelawny, looking for something to do and feeling pity for the ducks and geese broiling in their coops on deck, was moved to open the doors and liberate them. With glad quacks and squawks the birds landed in the water: the dogs splashed joyously after them, barking like lunatics: the crew let out a cheer and Byron, with the brave scarlet waistcoat in his hands, determined to join the bathing party. With one arm in the waistcoat he called, "Hi, Edward! put your arm in also. We will jump overboard and take the shine out of it."

So they did.

A cheer rent the air as they hit the water, cut off suddenly as the corpulent figure of the captain appeared at the head of the companionway. Cackling geese, barking dogs and laughing sailors made enough of a din to raise the dead: but when the captain looked overboard, saw the conjoined swimmers and realised the ruin of his favourite garment, his roar easily rose above the lot.

"Mylord!" he bellowed in anguish. "You should know better than to make a mutiny on board ship! I won't heave to or lower a boat! I hope you will both be drowned!"

"Then who will pay for our passage?" yelled Byron gleefully.

"You have ruined my waistcoat! It will be shrunk beyond hope!"

"Like Trelawny's mustachios!" carolled his lordship.

The poor man was dancing with rage and mortification. Trelawny, deciding that enough was enough, clambered back on board, dripping mustachios and all, and by dint of persuasion, coaxing and the hint of a bribe, induced him to put out a boat to collect the scattered fowls. It said much for Byron's powers of persuasion and the captain's innate good nature that their former friendly relations were restored: but ever after, the blunt sailor doubted his noble passenger's sanity, and he said as much to Fletcher as they shared a friendly "wet" together.

"Why is he going to such a wild country of savages? My Mate was at Corfu, and he says an officer of the garrison crossed over to Albania to shoot, and was shot himself; they thought his brass buttons were of gold."

"When I was there," said Fletcher, "the Turks were masters and kept them down. They live in holes in the rocks and come out like foxes, with guns and knives. We had to have a guard of soldiers wherever we went."

The captain's eyes popped. "How did you live?" he asked.

"Like dogs, sitting on the floor, eating out of one dirty round dish, tearing the meat with our fingers. They have a very vile potion they call wine, though it tastes more like turpentine, carried about in stinking goatskins, and all drink from the same bowl. They smoke when they don't sleep: they sleep in all their clothes: they don't wash: they are lousy. If the Turks go, it will be bedlam. Greece is a land of lice and flies and fleas and thieves. What Mylord is going there for the Lord only knows. *I* don't."

He realised they were no longer alone: Byron and Trelawny had come up behind them and had heard part at least of Fletcher's tirade. He looked Byron in the eye and added defensively: "My master can't deny that what I have said is true."

"No," said Byron, "to those who can see nothing else. What Fletcher says may be true, but I didn't note it. The Greeks are returned to barbarism, nor do I know what I am going for. I liked Greece and the London Committee told me I should be of use, but what use they did not say, nor do I see."

He turned away: his shoulders drooped; it seemed that all the old melancholy and uncertainty had returned. But the mood passed as they drew nearer to Greece with its past memories and present difficulties. In a rosy sunset they came at last to journey's end, sailing between the islands of Zante and Cephalonia: the old tub had brought them safely after all. Before them lay the distant mountains of the Morea, purple and peaceful in the evening light. Byron drew a deep sigh, and pulled the cloak closer round his shoulders. "I don't know why it is, Edward," he said softly, "but I feel as if the twelve long years of bitterness I have passed through since I was here were taken off my shoulders. I have come home!"

***

Argostoli was in a ferment. From mouth to mouth the message ran like wild fire: "Byron is coming! No, Byron is *here*!" "He has brought guns – he has brought soldiers – he has brought money!" Above all, money. How much, nobody knew – but from hundreds of piastres it soon grew to thousands, nay, millions! Nothing could stop them now.

Colonel Charles Napier was not so sanguine. This admirable and experienced officer, widely travelled through Albania and Greece and Resident of Cephalonia, was very naturally regarded with suspicion and disparagement by his colleagues: Byron and Mavrocordato knew better. Even Trelawny admitted, grudgingly, that here was the true expert on Greece and Grecian affairs. So it was obvious that the Committee in London had little time for his explanations of how matters stood: and no wonder that he prayed the Lord to deliver him from them. He would go his own way and present himself and his expertise to Byron. He at least would be realistic. It was unfortunate that at the moment of Byron's arrival he should be absent from Argostoli. It could not be helped, but he was all the same impatient to return and confer with his lordship.

Byron was sorry too, but could only possess his soul in patience. The reports he had from all sides were conflicting, and he would make no move until Colonel Napier returned to give him a true account. That he would trust. Meanwhile, it was not unpleasant to lie at anchor in the creek, looking at the whitewashed villas stuck as if with glue against the bare hillsides, listening to the distant noises of the town, with the smell of thyme wafted on the breeze. When night fell, the harbour lights spangled the dark water like tiny diamonds, and the echoing bugle calls of the English garrison stirred the blood. He slept like a baby, untroubled by the nightmares that had plagued his rest for so long, and was woken out of that deep, dreamless sleep by a crashing bump that nearly jerked him out of his narrow berth. It was followed by another, and another: sharp voices spoke rapidly in Greek: there was an oath, and a clatter above his head. Fully awake now, he dragged on his clothes and climbed on deck as swiftly as his limp would allow. A scene of the utmost confusion met his astonished gaze. A selection of whiskered ruffians in the well-remembered white skirts of the Suliotes were swarming over the rails and onto the deck, yelling encouragement to each other with cries of "Byron! Greece for ever!" His servant Lega had, with immense presence of mind and a nice sense of priorities, leaped on to the money-chest and lay there, "coiled like a viper", as Byron afterwards described it, prepared to sell his life dearly in its defence: and the captain, practical joking forgiven and forgotten, had seized a marlin-spike and was preparing to repel boarders, roaring at his amazed and reluctant crew to follow his example. The Greeks took no notice of either. They had spotted Byron, standing quietly at the top of the companion-way, playing with his handkerchief in his characteristic way, and rushed over to kneel at his feet and claim his protection. It was an emotive moment, which his lordship enjoyed hugely: but by the next day the novelty had worn thin, since they followed him about wherever he went like zealous and over-grateful mongrels. At last, quite exhausted, he turned to Trelawny for help.

"Edward, you are at home in seaports – for God's sake go ashore and find some vessel to take this crew away and maroon them somewhere. My head is reeling. I must have some peace!"

Trelawny was amused, but willing. "Where shall we maroon them?" he asked.

"Timbuctoo for all I care. No – I have it! They shall all go ahead and await us on the mainland. Tell them they are to be the advance guard. Your whiskers are much more fearsome than theirs are – they will do as you say. Only remove them, that's all I ask."

"It's your own fault – you have promised them much, and now they expect more."

"I can't help that. I can't do with them here, that's certain. You will arrange it admirably. Don't let yourself be milked though – our war-chest isn't bottomless."

Trelawny grinned, and went off on his errand. If Byron had suspected that Trelawny had over-estimated his powers of organization, he was proved wrong in this instance: all was arranged with the utmost efficiency, and the Suliotes departed full of enthusiasm, touchingly proud of the confidence shown in them, and urging his lordships to follow them soon. The brig seemed very quiet after they had gone.

Next day, Colonel Napier returned, and roared with laughter when he heard of this adventure. "That is typical of them," he said soberly, when his mirth had spent itself. "They are so full of optimism, and because of one or two small successes they believe not that the war may eventually be won but that victory is absolutely assured. But the Turks are not really trying at present: they are only playing at soldiers. If they really wanted to they could crush our Greeks tomorrow – no, today! They lack money, and the shipowners won't let the fleet sail without payment: the civil authorities quarrel with the military, each being afraid of losing face: *you* try telling them what happens to divided houses – they won't listen to me!"

"I'm not surprised," answered Byron. "I like the Greeks – I always have. They are plausible rogues and merry ones, but far too volatile. What's worse, they have acquired the vices of the Turks without their virtues – whatever one may think of the Turks, they do not lack courage. I shall not act hastily. I've come too far to take false steps."

The colonel nodded. "You are very wise! Stay here until the news is more reliable – and more encouraging. The whole affair has fallen into the doldrums. Why don't you come ashore and set up your headquarters at the residency? You will be very welcome – and much more comfortable!"

Byron shook his head.

"You're very kind, but I think I should stay here. There might be complications, and I must be ready to move at a moment's notice if need be."

"You may be right. But don't hesitate to make use of me if you think I can assist you in any way. And remember that there are beds for you and Count Gamba whenever you want them."

Byron did stay on board, almost, at first, as if he were a recluse, and when he received an invitation from the officers of the English garrison to dine with them his first impulse was to refuse it. Convinced as he was that all Englishmen looked upon him with contempt and loathing, and that professional fighting men would despise him as an amateur (and a crippled one at that!) he shrank from their robust company. A moment's reflection, however, told him that the invitation would hardly have been sent out of mere politeness, and he sent a gracious acceptance. He was glad he did. To his surprise and delight, the officers of the 8th Foot, the King's Regiment, welcomed him with respect and admiration. It was so long since his countrymen had regarded him with such emotions, so long since he had enjoyed an evening in their company, that Byron was quite overwhelmed. To his amazement he found that the more lurid aspects of his life troubled them not a whit: it was as the author of *Don Juan* that they regarded him with admiration – even with envy. It was intoxicating for a lonely man to feel wanted, and by his own kind: and he said so. "I'm a black sheep, you know," he said, smiling sadly. "But truly I am not as black as some have painted me, and I hope you will believe me and judge me as you find me, not merely by report." Colonel Duffie shifted in his chair.

"Well, well, Mylord," he said, "there can be hardly a man of us here around this table whose secrets would all bear exposure! but only one of us can produce a 'Lara' or a 'Corsair'! 'O'er the glad waters of the dark blue sea, Our thoughts as boundless and our souls as free!' Capital stuff, Mylord! Come, gentlemen!" he continued, rising to his feet. "I'll give you a toast! To the good health and genius of our distinguished guest, Lord Byron!"

"Lord Byron! Lord Byron!" responded the officers, and Byron rose to his feet, flushed and delighted, particularly bright of eye.

"Gentlemen," he said in his soft voice, as they resumed their seats. "I cannot find words adequately to express to you my thanks for your hospitality and kindness – and, I hope, your friendship. And, to tell the truth, I am doubtful whether I can express my sense of obligation as I ought, for I have been so long in the practice of speaking a foreign language that it is with some difficulty that I can hope to convey the whole force of what I feel in my own. So may I, gentlemen, simply say 'Thank you'?"

He could, and was applauded. Bright-eyed and blushing, he sat down, and leaning towards Colonel Duffie asked, "Was that all right? Did I do properly?" He felt suddenly shy and immensely happy. The whole mess rowed back to the brig with him and they parted on the most cordial of terms. He was blinking back unashamed tears when Fletcher came to put him to bed. "Like the prodigal son," he said, "I have had the fatted calf killed for me. I shall sleep well tonight."

Sleep well he did, but the morning brought fresh vexations and uncertainties. There was still no news from Missolonghi: no intelligence of Marco Botzaris' whereabouts, and until the messengers arrived he could do no more. He felt that to cool his heels, inactive in Argostoli, would fret him to screaming point. He would, he decided, have a holiday – he would spend the waiting time on an expedition. "We will follow Odysseus," he said to the devoted Pietro Gamba. "He too was a wandering outcast and his island is just across the strait. We will journey into Ithaca."

So, acting characteristically on impulse, he assembled his retinue and, mounted on mule-back, they rose across Cephalonia to the opposite coast. Byron was like a boy let out of school: he was too impatient to delay his trip by so much as one night, and disdaining all offers of hospitality embarked the whole party in a rowing-boat. His high spirits were infectious, and by the time they ground on the beach of Ithaca everyone, including the three servants, was shouting and singing. Trelawny had started a lusty shanty, and even Dr Bruno, who knew none of the English words, could join in with a hearty "Tra-la!" It was now sunset, and the song faded into silence as the party realised that here they were on a bare and rocky coast with no habitation in sight and nightfall at hand. Byron, whose mood was still rollicking, was for sleeping out in one of the caves among the cliffs: but Pietro, who was less adventurous in spirit, volunteered to go in search of a hospitable householder. No one believed he would find any such thing, but luck was with him, and in little more than an hour he came scrambling back down to the beach accompanied by an excitable – and voluble – gentleman who insisted that the whole party should spend the night under his roof. It was a very small roof, but all the same they crammed in and were pressed to partake of all that the household had to offer. Their host was effusive – too effusive – and Byron's uplifted mood collapsed under a weight of verbiage.

"You cannot conceive, Milor', how privileged my wife" (a plump and smiling, silent woman – well she might be, thought Byron savagely: she could never expect to get a word in sideways!) "feels to welcome you here to our humble cottage. I apologise for that – it was not always so, and it is not what your lordship is accustomed to. Ah, dear, I was not always a poor man – in Trieste my name was an honoured one but these troublous times take their toll and none knows what might befall tomorrow. When Greece is free of her oppressors – with your lordship's help – there may be a different tale to tell! Then we shall come into our own again, be very sure! The cause is a noble one and worthy of your lordship's utmost endeavours. Pray take some more wine! No, no, I insist," (filling his lordship's glass to the brim) "we shall all drink to the resurrection of Greece and defiance to the Sultan! But your lordship is more than welcome and I can guess – haha! I can guess! – what brings you to Ithaca. You, a poet, could not rest without following in Homer's footsteps – you must see for yourself the ways that Odysseus trod! You will be inspired! Your Muse will be excited! And where better could you be placed? Above us on the hilltop is Odysseus' own castle! We can show you the grotto of the Nymphs – the very fountain to Arethusa! Your lordship will dip therein and your poetic genius will be refreshed. It cannot be otherwise!"

He prattled on. Byron, irritated by all this fulsomeness, muttered to Trelawny, "I feel stifled! I detest antiquarian twaddle. Do people really think that I came to Greece to scribble more nonsense? If so, I wish I had never written a line. Come out into the garden with me – let us take a turn in the cool – to cool me off!"

Trelawny was willing enough: the cool night air, the sea sparkling under the stars and a ready listener soon restored Byron's equilibrium. He said "I'm sorry, Edward. The man meant well, but oh! How I loathe such prattle! Out here it is so different. Look at those silent islands – how peaceful, how serene, how timeless! I am soothed already."

Trelawny said carefully, "Your lordship has too much on your mind. This waiting is enough to nag at any man."

Byron laughed, a short, bitter laugh. "I have had too much on my mind for years. But to be here among such magnificent scenery brings me real happiness. I feel as if I had never been away. It was love at first sight when I first came to Greece – so many years ago! And it is the one love that has lasted. As a youth I knew discomfort here, anger, sickness, disappointment. But I was always happy."

Trelawny said nothing.

The soft voice continued. "We had great times, you know, Hobhouse and I. We slept in palaces – and in hovels. We shared our quarters with noblemen – and with farm animals. We survived tempests and earthquakes. We were nearly ship-wrecked – nearly captured by brigands – I nearly died of fever. But I was always happy. And I wanted – even then – to do something for Greece, to repay something of what she had done for me. I remember a man who begged that his people's taxes should be reduced. Do you know, Edward, that poor village was asked for seven hundred pounds? Seven hundred pounds – and more – from peasants! I promised to speak to Ali Pasha myself on their behalf, and they were so grateful. And I did ask, but I never discovered if my efforts had been of any use, so whether they prospered or starved I never knew. And I should have known! My intentions were of the best, but I was young and foolish and forgot – until many years later. Too late – that is the story of my life, isn't it?"

Trelawny's cheroot glowed red in the darkness. He said carefully, "It is never too late, Mylord, in this world – or so they say. You are here to repay the debt – if debt there be – and nothing can change that!"

Byron sighed. "Well! I must banish ill-humour and be patient. Maybe tomorrow will bring us news."

***

The morrow brought no fresh intelligence, and Byron was not altogether displeased. His intended holiday would not be interrupted after all, and he set off as planned to the home of the Resident at Vathi, one Captain Knox. Their way led them, as promised, past the Castle of Odysseus, with its cavern and its grotto: one look was enough to inform Byron that his leg would not permit him to climb so far, and with resignation he sat himself in the grotto with a book while the more active members of the party attempted the ascent. The sun was hot, the grass springy and scented beneath his fingers, and the gentle splash or dropping water within the grotto lulled his senses. The book dropped from his lap: his head fell back against the turf, and Byron slept. Pietro Gamba, scrambling back down the bank, thought he had never seen such a look of peace on his courtesy brother-in-law's face. It seemed a pity to wake him, but time was getting on and so must they. "Bairon!" he cried, shaking his lordship by the shoulder. "Wake up! Time to go on!" and felt a cad for doing so.

"Curse you!" said his lordship, but good-naturedly. "I could have slept here for ever! You woke me from the pleasantest dream I ever had in my life: and now it has gone." He would not say more, but the cloud had returned, and Pietro was sorry for it. It was, he felt, his fault, and he welcomed the plan made for the next morning when they were to visit the Fountain of Arethusa.

But to the consternation of everyone, there was no sign of Byron in the morning. He was not in his room, and Gamba's perturbation was not helped by Trelawny, who emerged from his own room with the intelligence that his lordship had not seemed well during the night and had gone out very early. Everyone looked troubled and Captain Knox was debating where best to search for his distinguished guest when he was seen coming up from the beach towards the house, looking like a ghost. He was leaning heavily on a stick as he walked slowly along, his head bent, eyes fixed on the ground. Captain Knox was horrified, but his lordship would not suffer any putting-off of the expedition and shrugged off all suggestions that he should rest awhile. "No, no," he said, "I am quite well, I assure you. I have been writing half the night and have been for a swim, which always does me good." And "So much," thought Trelawny, for the non-inspiration of his muse!" Pietro felt unhappy and guilty. He remembered how Byron, deserted by them all, had gone to sleep in the sun. Could it have had ill-effects? He took an early opportunity of consulting the doctor. Bruno looked grave.

"It could be so, Conte. If I had only known! But he did not mention this. He complained a little of the headache, that is all, and I prescribed for him some little pills which he has taken before with the most beneficial effects. I see he has his cap on his head, and I will take care to see he wears it always. His constitution is not strong, that I know – but he has a burning flame!"

True to his word, the little doctor kept a close eye on Byron all day: but he was back in spirits and for the rest of his short holiday gave no more cause for alarm to any of his followers.

It did not last. On their return to Cephalonia, they were to stay the night at the monastery of Sami, where the monks were apparently in a high state of excitement at the prospect. Byron, who contrary to his usual custom had eaten a large dinner, said nothing in answer to this information: he looked pale and grim, but set out in silence. They could hardly miss the way: the path to the monastery was lined with holy men carrying torches of pine whose flames danced over their faces and gave them the appearance of hobgoblins. More monks crowded the terrace as the party approached, chanting in chorus a specially composed welcome. "Christ has risen!" they intoned, "To elevate the Cross and trample on the Crescent in our beloved Greece!" There was more in the same vein: the Abbot himself, in ceremonial robes, came with outstretched hands to greet his lordship, and ushered him with glad respect into the great hall. The blaze of light within made Byron blink: the serving boys swung their censers under his nose: the monks crowded round: and the Abbot, delving into his draperies and bringing out an immense scroll from their folds, launched into a flowery encomium.

Trelawny, biting his lips, was hard put to it not to burst out laughing. Sure that his lordship would share the joke he managed to catch his eye, and almost staggered back at the flash of fury that he saw in Byron's expression. Unable to contain himself any longer, Byron let loose a torrent of enraged Italian, consigning the Abbot, the monks and all their works, singly and collectively, to the nethermost pit and a particularly pitiless devil. Then he turned on Trelawny. "Will no one," he cried, "release me from the presence of these pestilential idiots? They drive me mad!" and seizing one of the candelabra, he limped hastily out of the hall.

There was a stricken silence: the unfortunate Abbot, halted in mid-peroration with his mouth open, looked aghast. Gamba stepped hastily into the breach, excusing the inexcusable, explaining that his lordship was tired and ailing, having been exposed too long to the hot sun, and with much on his mind. The Abbot, only slightly appeased, stared at him: then slowly nodded, and putting a finger to his head said in a trembling voice: "I understand – the poor man is mad!"

Horrified, Gamba attempted to disabuse him of this misconception, but the Abbot remained unconvinced and was more than ever certain of his diagnosis in the morning. It was a dreadful night, and one which everyone hoped to forget with all possible speed. While the rest of the party were sitting quietly in the salon, after this most uncomfortable evening, they were startled out of their seats by Dr Bruno, who came rushing in, calling upon the Virgin, wringing his hands and tearing his hair like a madman himself. It was Trelawny who brutally and effectively shook the doctor by the shoulders and demanded to know the reason for this irruption.

"Stop it!" he commanded. "Calm yourself at once – you do no good by all this hullabaloo and *we* cannot help if we do not know the matter. Is it his lordship?"

Bruno, his eyes popping out of his head, gulped and nodded. "I can do nothing with him!" he declared. "He has dreadful pains – but dreadful pains – here!" He clutched his stomach dramatically. "He stamps about and tears off his clothes! He is inflamed in body and mind! He is in such pain – such pain – but he will not take my medicines! He will not let me near him! He must have physic – he must be purged – and I cannot make him! Help me! Oh help me!"

Trelawny's eyes narrowed. "*I* see what it is!" he said. "Touch of the sun, indeed! It is that enormous dinner, and all the quantity of wine that went down with it! Leave him to me!" and off he strode, his bristling eyebrows and flashing dark eyes making him look more like a bird of prey than ever. He was back in no time, baffled and exasperated. "I cannot control him!" he declared. "It will take ten men each as strong as I to hold him. At present he seems bent on smashing everything in sight. Listen!"

A distant banging seemed to bear out the truth of this. The poor little doctor was almost beside himself, darting about in an agony. "But one little pill!" he moaned. "He will thank us when he is well. One little pill, and he will be safe!" The whole party, now seriously alarmed, trooped up to Byron's room. He had barricaded himself in with all the furniture it held, but there was no lock on the door and it yielded easily. Byron had retreated into a corner at the sound of their coming: like an animal at bay he snarled at them "Fiends! can I have no peace, no relief from this hell? Leave me!" He swayed a moment on the balls of his feet: then crossing the room in a rush he seized a chair and hurled it straight at them. Fortunately, they saw it coming in time: Byron followed up his advantage and slammed the door again. It shivered on its hinges, but held. They were left staring at the blank panels.

They withdrew along the corridor, and a whispered consultation took place. It was Hamilton-Browne who saved the situation. "I think you were wrong," he said to Trelawny. "Too many of us at once will only make him worse: one of us might be able to reason with him. Let us see if a soft answer will turn away wrath."

"Yours, I suppose," muttered Trelawny. He felt chagrined that his own robust methods had met with no success.

"Yes, mine. Give me your pills, Doctor, and we'll see if he can be persuaded to swallow them."

"Here, sir, here! This one – and this – they will reduce the cramps and then he will sleep like a babe unborn. But have a care!"

"I will be wary," promised Hamilton-Browne. "We won't be too far away," said Trelawny. "Be ready to call if you need assistance. He has the strength of ten devils at present."

They retreated in good order, and waited, on the alert for any sounds of battle. None came: there was an ominous silence, even more alarming than the previous racket. Then the door opened quietly: Hamilton-Browne emerged, serene and unruffled. He closed it gently behind him, and came tiptoeing along the corridor. "You may rest easy, Dr Bruno," he said to the anxious physician. "His lordship has taken both your pills and is now tucked up in bed."

"Heaven be praised!" gasped the doctor. "How did you manage it, sir?"

"To tell the truth, there was very little for me to do," said Hamilton-Browne. "By the time I returned his lordship's legs had given way beneath him and as he was already half-undressed it was not so difficult as I had feared. I'm afraid he will have a headache in the morning." He grinned disarmingly. "It must be a very potent liquor they brew in these parts," he said. "May it be a warning to us all."

He was right. Byron appeared next morning pale and penitent. "Oh, my head!" he muttered. "My head! What have I done to deserve this?"

"Too much!" retorted Trelawny roughly. "You were fighting mad last night and I do not believe the unfortunate Abbot will ever forgive you. How could you upset him so? I fear you have lost his goodwill for ever."

"I remember now," said Byron. "I was drunk, you know."

"Yes, I do know! Though at first we thought you ill and the Abbot thought you mad. You will have to beg his pardon, you know. Whether he will grant it to you remains to be seen."

So Byron dutifully went off to make his peace with the Abbot. He did not particularly enjoy the interview and it was in a mood of black dejection that he started off on the ride back to Argostoli. The moors and marshes were not calculated to raise his spirits but Byron's restless temperament could not be gloomy for long when on the move. As his headache lightened, so did his mood, and he started to sing.

"The Minstrel Boy," he carolled, "to the war has gone,
In the ranks of death you'll find him.
His father's sword he has girded on
And his wild harp slung behind him!"

"Oh, rare Tom Moore! shall we ever meet again? The minstrel has gone to the war but the war seems loth to come to the minstrel!" His voice rose again, and his companions caught up the chorus.

"'Land of song' said the warrior bard,
'Tho' all the world betrays thee,
One sword at least thy rights shall guard,
One faithful harp shall praise thee'!"

Night had fallen by the time they reached Argostoli. Singing and laughing they came on board the brig, all disharmony forgotten, though Dr Bruno shook his head and looked grave. And when they arrived, Byron found at last that some letters had arrived too.

***

The long-awaited letter from Marco Botzaris, encamped among the mountains of Agrapha, had arrived. Byron turned up the lamp and read it avidly.

"Your letter, and that of the venerable Ignazio, have filled me with joy. Your Excellency is exactly the person of whom we stand in need. Let nothing prevent you from coming into this part of Greece. The enemy threatens us in great number: but by the help of God and your Excellency they shall meet a suitable resistance. I shall have something to do to-night against a corps of six or seven thousand Albanians, encamped close to this place. The day after to-morrow I will set out with a few chosen companions, to meet your Excellency. Do not delay. I thank you for the good opinion you have of my fellow-citizens, which God grant you will not find ill-founded: and I thank you still more for the care you have so kindly taken of them."

The letter was dated 18th August: it was now the 22nd, and there had been no further news of the attack mentioned by Botzaris. The night had been dark: Botzaris in his tent at Carpenisi had sealed his letter and handed it straight to the messenger who, he thought, would have no difficulty in getting back to Argostoli without mishap. For himself, he intended to rest before the time came. He took off his boots and stretched himself out, wrapped in his huge Albanian-style cloak: soon he fell into a light and restful slumber.

His lieutenant trod softly into the tent some three hours later, and laid a hand on his shoulder. Botzaris was awake on the instant. He started up, reaching out for his boots. "Is it time?"

"It is time, my general. All is ready: we but await your commands!"

Botzaris was dragging on his boots. "I will give them myself. What have the scouts to tell?"

"We must be swift and sure, my general. Omar Pasha himself is in the enemy camp: they number some eight thousand to our hundreds. Surprise will be all."

Botzaris nodded. "Surprise and silence."

The lieutenant answered, "It is understood, General."

"It is well."

The two men left the tent, and walked together to the edge of the campsite, where the ranks of partisans were drawn up in order. Botzaris ran his eye over them, and was satisfied. "The hour is come," he said. "I will go before, and you will follow every man close at a comrade's heels. There must be no noise: let every man be sure to keep his weapon loaded, but no one must fire until I give the word. We must be in their midst before they are aware. When I brandish my sabre, we will charge!"

Like panthers, the troop set off into the darkness, moving silently but surely, each man totally familiar with the terrain. The band came to a halt after some half-hour's march, at Botzaris's lifted hand. The enemy camp was now in plain view: a sentry was pacing back and forth, his musket slung across his shoulder. Botzaris, in the shadows, raised a finger: in answer, a brawny sergeant padded stealthily to his side, one eyebrow cocked. No word passed between the two men. Botzaris pointed silently to the sentry: the sergeant nodded intelligently, and next instant had melted into the darkness. Not even his own men saw the way he went: but where one moment one man had paced along the perimeter a shadow crept along behind him. Something flashed in the darkness, quicker than thought: the sentry crumpled where he stood, without a sound, and was swiftly dragged out of sight.

Botzaris sighed: the sergeant materialised out of the night, and two muskets hung from his shoulder. The long knife was still in his hand, the bright edge dulled: his eyes gleamed. The column formed again and the stalk continued. Once a twig crackled under an unwary boot: everyone halted as if frozen, not daring to breathe: but there was no sound of alarm from the enemy, and they carried on undisturbed.

They were now within ten paces of the enemy lines. Botzaris raised his sabre above his head in the pre-arranged signal. With blood-curdling yells, half the brigade charged the tents where the Albanians lay: the rest, on one knee, covered those tents with their muskets, ready to fire at anyone who emerged. In an instant, the field was alive with half-dressed and wild-eyed men: sabres flashed, muskets cracked and the screams of the wounded, the moans of the dying, mingled with savage howls of rage and triumph. The surprise had been complete: the Albanian force, superior in numbers though they were, were taken wholly unaware and lay in tangled heaps across the battlefield.

The heroic band of Suliots, inspired by patriotic fervour, followed close at Botzaris's heels: the stricken dropped as they ran, ignored by their fellows, who kept on with one aim in mind, to reach the tent of the Pasha himself. They had all but reached their goal when a great cry of despair rose above the tumult, and the lieutenant was seen bending over the body of Botzaris. He had fallen on the instant, shot in the head: the ball had penetrated to the brain and he had had no time even to cry out. The remnants of the Suilot army, with victory in their grasp, bereft of their leader, fell back across the tangled piles of dead. It was with some ado that they were able to carry away their leader's body, but carry it they did to be buried with all honours at Missolonghi, where Botzaris and Byron had hoped to rendezvous. Even as Byron read of this promise in the harbour at Argostoli, Botzaris had been four days dead. The Albanians had suffered a real setback, routed as they were, with many of their leading officers dead at Carpenisi, they withdrew in good order: but Missolonghi was still blockaded from the sea by the Turkish fleet, and his lordship's plans had all to be recast.

His first impulse was to head immediately for the Morea to take stock of the situation, but wiser counsels prevailed. The little *Hercules* was no fit craft to rush the Turkish blockade, and the captain was, not surprisingly, reluctant to risk either his vessel or himself in such an enterprise. And clearly it would not do to make her a permanent headquarters. All in all, it seemed most sensible to send her back to England and to cast about for some more suitable lodging on land. Trelawny was impatient of all this caution: he had come to Greece to see some action, and action he intended to have.

"I do not understand you," he raged. "All this plotting, planning, shillyshallying and in the end doing nothing. You see what has come of it! We were recommended to two leaders: and here we have Botzaris dead and Mavrocordato skedaddled. Refugee forsooth!" His hawk's eyes flashed with contempt. "Well, if you will not set out now, I will!"

"You must do as you think fit," Byron answered placidly. "I see little good in proceeding at present. I must learn the real state of affairs and make myself familiar to those with influence, if I am to have any success in settling their discords. Also, remember I have the privilege of providing the war-chest – if that is lost, all is lost!"

Trelawny snorted. "Afraid?" he asked.

Byron remained unmoved. "No," he said, "not afraid, but prudent. You do not know the Greeks – I know them, I think, as well as any outside Greece! And the worst of them is that they are such damned liars! I will make no definite move until I have arrived at the truth." He paused, then went on, more quietly, "You know, when first I went to Athens, so many years ago, I found them much attached to their own nation. They would publicly express their loathing of the Turks in a way that seemed downright foolhardy. Yet if you urged them to action they would cringe and say, "What can I do?" Now, I do not intend to be foolhardy and I know what I can do – thus much and no more! I will walk dryshod over the morass and come out safe the other side: I will be careful to make not one false step. There's your answer."

"Well, it will not do for me! I am for the Morea! And Brown comes with me."

"You must do as you think best," Byron repeated. "If you are determined, perhaps you would be so good as to take a letter to the Government for me: an answer to that will assist my own decisions."

"Oh, certainly! I will be your postman if you have no more martial orders for me."

On that note they parted, Trelawny to head for the war zone, Byron to resolve the conflicting demands being made upon him. They never saw each other again.

So Byron bided his time, and it was fully a month before his representations to the Government were answered. He spent the time agreeably enough, having found a suitable base in the little village of Metaxata some four miles inland. Here in a whitewashed cottage heavily draped with ivy he could sit on the balcony and make plans at his leisure. The four rooms of the top floor made a comfortable if crowded home: Byron was snug enough with a bedroom and sitting-room all to himself, but Pietro and Dr Bruno had to share an apartment while the servants made shift for themselves in the kitchen. It was an idyllic spot, more suited to the poet than the politician: war seemed far removed from this peaceful nook, backed by the mountains and fronted by the sea, with the scent of lemon and cypress all around. Theirs was a simple life, but hardly lonely: all manner of visitors came to call and there was no lack of company. To Colonel Napier, who brought news out of England, he was always willing to talk: and to listen to what he had to tell of the world his lordship had left behind for ever.

"You know, Colonel," he said, "I am reckoned a black sheep – yet, after all, not so black as the world believes me." The Colonel made no answer, and Byron went on, "Would you believe I could be more sinned against than sinning?"

"That could be said of most men, Mylord."

"Exactly. I saw the traps and walked straight into them – now call me a fool! 'Thou shalt not be found out' is excellent rede – if you can abide by it. I was always fond of feminine company, you see."

"That is self-evident!" said Napier with a twinkle.

"Oh, not like that! or at least, not at the beginning like that. Man and woman are a balance, you know: it is a poor kind of society that sets one against the other, that professes one to be superior, when in fact we are two halves of the whole. But women are strange creatures: they are not content to share a part of a man: they must hold him utterly, body and soul."

He crossed to the table, and poured out two more glasses of wine. Handing one to his guest, he went on. "So! I have been called mad, bad and dangerous to know – but the madness was momentary, the badness was imaginary, and the danger – was brought upon themselves." He sank back into his chair, and stretched out his legs. "Let me ask you, Colonel, one question – and by your answer you shall judge me! If a pretty girl had chased you half across a continent and up a mountain to boot until she caught you – what would you have done?"

Napier smiled. "Precisely what you did, Mylord – I would suppose."

"You would suppose right – and I am answered. Had I been a hardened reprobate, the world's censure would be easier to bear: indeed, I would not care two straws about it. But I am not hard, you see, nor reprobate by design. How it happened I am not quite sure – one thing led to another, you see. I was an

ardent youth, consumed with the desire to be a great poet. I
don't claim to be one: all the same, I woke one morning to find
myself famous. That's heady stuff, you know – to be fêted,
courted, pursued even: and time after time when I thought I
was wanted for myself I found it was not I, not even my poetry –
only my fame. Once I thought I had met the one woman who
could have saved me from myself – but she would not have me
when I wanted, and when she did have me – I no longer wanted
her. Strange. Even I cannot tell you why."

Greatly daring, Napier asked, "Lady Byron?"

"Lady Byron. Poor thing, she never could understand me, nor
I her: so today you find me the loneliest of outcasts, Ishmael in
the wilderness: friendless, wifeless, childless. No, I am *not*
growing maudlin: I have had but two glasses and yours, I see,
is empty again." He refilled it. "I had a little daughter – did you
know? Such a funny, solemn little thing: but she died. She died.
Why she should suffer for my punishment I do not know, nor
ever shall. There is my little legitimacy: she still lives, but must
be dead to me for ever. I shall not be allowed to see her in this
life."

The soft voice had not risen, nor broken: Napier sat very still,
not daring to say a word. Byron raised his head, smiling crookedly. "So – I have bared my soul to you, Napier – I wonder why?
Catharsis is good for a man's soul, they say. I could never have
talked so to anyone closer: but there is no one closer, nor is there
ever likely to be again. And here I am, as you see me. I hope I
may yet do some good in this world!"

Napier said carefully, "That hope is strong in many, Mylord:
here at least you are wanted and welcome."

Byron sighed. "True – and I wish that the day of action were
at hand to give me no time for thought. Yet I like this place – I
do not know why – and dislike to move. There are not, to be
sure, many allurements here: there is no learned society, nor
the presence of beautiful women: and yet, for all that, I would
wish to remain, as I have found myself more comfortable, and
my time passes more cheerfully, than it has for long done."

So he stayed, most wisely, building up both his own strength
and his knowledge of affairs: and so September passed.

***

Byron had not been wholly honest when he spoke of the cheerful passage of time. The baring of his soul to Colonel Napier had had its immediate origin in disturbing news from England about his "little legitimacy": Ada had been ill, quite ill, and the conviction he had of never seeing his daughter in this life came as much from a fear of her death as from a premonition of his own. She had suffered, so he was given to understand, a "determination of blood to the head," and he reproached himself as bequeathing this as his legacy to the child he did not know. He mentioned this fear, not to Napier but to his medical attendant: and his fears were only partially soothed by the brisk rejoinder that that was hardly surprising, considering the way he pored over his books at all hours of the day and night – indeed, Mylord had an inflamed eye at this moment! What did he expect? His lordship couldn't answer, but in his heart he felt more outcast than ever, longing for some means of being again reconciled with his wife, of getting to know and love his daughter, of asking their forgiveness. Then Teresa's image would rise again before him, and another restless night would make the headache worse. The web of his life was too tangled: it must be cut, and begun again.

Then there were the Greeks, whom he admired and scorned in the same breath: half-civilised, vicious, brave and vacillating at the same time. He remembered his old acquaintance Ali Pasha and his condemnation of them: there was some justification in his strictures, but he had brutalised them into submission. Byron hoped that example might show them a better way. There were times when that hope grew dim, and he felt that if he had power over them he would pave the roads with them, such barbarians they showed themselves to be. He said as much in utter exasperation when one day a party of navvies was buried by a fall of earth in the trench they were digging for one of the roads with which Napier meant to improve the island. Byron immediately sent Dr Bruno to render what aid he could, and started off afterwards himself as soon as his horse could be saddled. He did not have to ask the way: the high keening of women led him straight to the spot. A scene of utter confusion met his horrified gaze. The whole trench had collapsed: a handful of stout workmen were leaning on their shovels, watching with detached interest as Dr Bruno, single-handed, moved among the groaning figures of those few they had dug from the wreckage. There did not seem to be very many of them. Byron rode up to the tallest and strongest of the labourers, and demanded urgently: "Where are the rest of your comrades? Are there any more under the ground?"

The other turned slowly around and considered. "Ay," he said indifferently. "I believe so. There may be – or there may be not. Who knows?"

"Buried alive! And you do nothing! You idle rogue, give me your spade!" and springing as nimbly as he could from the saddle he snatched it from the man's hand and began frantically to dig. No one else moved: they watched with interest to see what he would do next. What he did do surprised them: for he flung down the spade, snatched up his whip and threatened to lay it about their lazy sides if they did not follow his example. "I will flay every one if need be!" he cried. "And you will not rest until every man is brought out, dead or alive!"

The men muttered, but obeyed. Reluctantly they set to on their grisly task, but the women clung around Byron's knees and blessed him, while the children stood wide-eyed, fingers in their mouths, wondering at all the rumpus.

In his disgust, Byron came within an ace of abandoning his whole enterprise: but the black mood lifted, and by the time October came in he was once more impatient for news. To Teresa he had written that he was a fool to have come, but being there must see what was to be done: he was coming round to the idea that there was little he could do, the Greeks themselves being rent with internal bickerings: that he was in fact wasting his time and substance: and that he might as well wash his hands of the whole affair and return to Italy. Teresa, eagerly reading his brief letters over and over again, allowed herself to hope against hope that this mood would prevail. Then suddenly, everything changed.

United for once in the face of the common enemy, the Greeks had encountered a Turkish squadron and seized Corinth. The news of this success had inspired the volatile islanders with rejoicing. Optimistic as ever, they were convinced that the war was as good as won, and danced by torchlight in the streets of Argostoli while Byron, realistic as ever, took literal account of the situation. He was relieved that Colonel Stanhope had returned to him with a true picture of the state of affairs, but as he had feared, the Colonel also brought news that the Greek Committee's own funds were exhausted.

"Is that certain?" he asked, not expecting the answer to be otherwise: Stanhope was too reliable a source.

"Too true, Mylord: mostly frittered away, some to this faction, some to that. But you are already aware of this."

"Yes. What fools they are, to be sure! Do you hear all that singing in the distance, Colonel? They are convinced that the war is won, when it is hardly even started. Does the Committee think a brigade can be formed, let alone sustained, without money? Well, I will myself negotiate a loan for their fleet, but they must learn not to squander it. With a loan they may do much, if they are sensible."

"Your lordship is more than generous."

He smiled a little crookedly. "I promised to help them and I won't – no, I *won't* – be forsworn! God knows it's little enough I have been able to do so far: and yet perhaps my time has not been entirely wasted, if we have managed at last to move the Deputies and made them pull together for once instead of in opposite directions – which can only result in a standstill."

Stanhope said, "You must admit, Mylord, that the news from Corinth has been a great source of encouragement."

"Oh, encouraging indeed! But Missolonghi is still in great peril, and Missolonghi is the key to the whole of the Morea. I hear that the Turks too have had their successes, and are amassed in the gulf in great force. That is a serious situation. I have half a mind to go to Tripolis myself for discussions with the Government, if I can dodge their roaming buccaneers! If only Mavrocordato would get his fleet to Missolonghi I should know how to proceed."

Stanhope said carefully, "If your lordship would trust me, I would be more than willing to take a letter to the Government stating your opinions and views on the situation. It would never do for your lordship to risk capture or worse in such an enterprise. But I would gladly tell them with all the force I can that there can be no more financial help from any quarter while the state of civil war continues."

Byron's look brightened. "Would you indeed? I will not say 'no' to such an offer. Good heavens, why can they not see that before they can conquer the Turks they must conquer themselves? I tell you what it is, there is more of the Levant in them than they realise! Victory is within their grasp, yet they will lose everything rather than lose face, each man aiming to be higher than his fellow. It will not do, and they *must* be made to realise it. The choice is theirs – to win their freedom, to become dependent on the rest of Europe – or to remain under the Turkish heel. And if they really wish for the first alternative, they must stop squabbling, or they will be slaves for ever."

"Well, that is a fine sermon, but you are preaching to the converted in me, Mylord! Tell *them* what you have just said! Write your letter, and I will undertake to deliver it."

So the letter was written, and in due course delivered. Byron waited in a fever of impatience for news from the war zone, torn between the desire for action and the promptings of his inner, wiser self. The news filtered through gradually – but the news was good. First there came intelligence of a naval coup: followed closely by naval farce. Things hadn't changed much in fifteen years, thought Byron, remembering the tragi-comedy of his voyage from Previsa. They had intercepted two Turkish vessels, laden with money and illustrious passengers – hurrah! There had been a fierce skirmish – ooh! The Turks had run aground and surrendered – hurrah! The Greeks, following enthusiastically, had run aground themselves. Oh, oh! Should one laugh or cry? The Turks made up their minds to retire with dignity: and Byron also made up his mind. At last, he would set out for Missolonghi and attempt to bring order to the confusion.

For despite the continued string of small successes, it was obvious that the various Greek parties had no intention of co-operating with each other: and the over-enthusiastic Stanhope was creating his own brand of mayhem. Mavrocordato's pleas became urgent, and could no longer be ignored. "You will be received here," he assured his lordship, "as a saviour. Be assured, Mylord, that it depends only on yourself to secure the destiny of Greece." Stanhope too was in a state of high excitement, though he managed to give the impression that his lordship's presence, though necessary, was not as necessary as the loan that would come through him, if mutiny among the unpaid fleet were to be avoided. All the same, "You are expected," he wrote, "with feverish anxiety. Your further delay in coming will be attended with serious consequences."

That settled it. His baggage had been prepared these many days, and Byron left his retreat immediately for Argostoli, to arrange his passage. Again he listened to the inner voice of caution, and lived to be grateful for it. He would not risk any Greek vessel, lawful prey of some marauding Turk: he would hire his own transport locally, and fly the flag of neutral Ionia. He would send his servants, the horses and the luggage in the larger of two while he himself and his immediate party would sail in a smaller, swifter vessel. Once galvanised into action, there was no hesitation – his orders were swift, sure and complete. His urgency communicated itself to everyone else, so much so that when word came from the heavy bombard that all was stowed and ready, Pietro Gamba was on board, equipped with a Bible and a telescope, before Byron even realised that he had left the house.

"Why, is Gamba gone?" he asked, in a voice of the utmost surprise. "He has carried with him all my money! But where is Fletcher?" No one knew. "Send someone after him – we must embark immediately! Send down to the mess-house – you will probably find him there taking a parting glass."

He guessed right: the errant Fletcher, glass in hand, was gloomily bidding farewell to the garrison. It was not the first nor yet the second glass, and the gloom was pronounced. "Think of me," he was urging, with a catch in his voice, "when you are snug in your dormitory: think of me, on a mud floor, beset by mosquitoes, having supped on addled eggs and lucky to have them: think of me among the barbarians! Mine is a cruel fate!" and he drank deeply.

"Why go then?" asked an interested sergeant.

"Why go? Because his lordship cannot do without me, that's why! There's no knowing what he would get up to without me – and I would never sleep sound at night for worrying over him."

"Are you so fond of him, then?"

"I love him," said Fletcher seriously, "as my own son. But I tell you this – it's a great pity he ever set foot in this God-forsaken country. I always said so, and I always will!" He looked up, as a panting messenger arrived, calling with what little breath he had left for "Mr Fletcher!"

"Here I am! What's up?"

"You're wanted aboard, sir. All's ready, and Mylord in afidget to be gone."

"I'm coming," said Fletcher deeply as he set down his empty glass. "Farewell, friends! You will never see me more."

It was a fine exit line, worthy of one of his master's own verse dramas. Fletcher was proud of it.

He arrived at the quay to find Byron already pacing about impatiently. Hampered and handicapped on land, his lordship was a changed man within sight and sound of the sea. In it or on it, his spirits rose, his cares fell away and he became a light-hearted boy again. So it was now. Even to be in the rowing-boat that took him out to the mystico where she lay at anchor in the creek sent his spirits soaring. He laughed and chaffed his companions, and especially the faithful valet whose miseries had already begun. A strong breeze was blowing: as the oars dipped into the water the spray came spattering up over the seat in the stern where Fletcher sat grimly, getting wetter and wetter by the minute. "Hi, Fletcher!" he called gaily, "You were busy wetting your inside when I wanted you – now see how your outside comes to match!" He clambered aboard the ship with surprising agility, with his drenched servitor stoically scrambling in his wake. He leant over the rail, extending his hand down to his erstwhile companions. "Farewell!" he cried. "If for ever, farewell – but I shall look to see you again soon – when we've chased the Turk back home!"

The sails rose and filled. Down below in the rowing boat Mr Hancock the banker and Mr Muir the doctor watched the two ships sail slowly out of the creek to the eastward, until they could no longer make out the figure on the smaller of the two who stood waving a handkerchief as the distance between them grew ever longer. At last their straining eyes could no longer pick out that fluttering white scrap. Then they turned, and rowed silently back to Argostoli.

***

It was a lovely evening for a sail. The wind was fresh, but not too strong, and even Pietro could enjoy the cruise, bad sailor though he was. The heat of the day had subsided into a delicious coolness, while the stars were so clear and bright it seemed that one had only to reach out a hand to pluck Cassiopeia from her chair. Aboard, there was almost a carnival atmosphere: the crews, with home over the horizon and a feeling of patriotic fervour in their breasts, launched into a chorus of Greek folk songs as they worked. One man would begin and his fellows joined in by twos and threes until the whole company was in full voice. The songs were neither gay nor rousing, but they were Greek, and that was enough. Even the Englishmen joined in: the infection was catching and Byron was in the most elevated of spirits, calling through cupped hands to Gamba in the other ship across the waters that divided them. But gradually the slower vessel fell farther and farther astern. His final call was: "Tomorrow we meet at Missolonghi – tomorrow!" Gamba fired off a pistol to show that he had heard and understood. The mystico sped on into the night, and silence fell.

The hours passed, and it had grown chilly in the long open ship. Byron, glad of his big cloak, wrapped it tightly around him. By now they had entered the Gulf: it was still dark, and somewhere ahead of them, not too far away, a flare suddenly rose into the sky and sputtered out. A moment or two later, nearer this time, came another, then another: it was all very puzzling. Then almost on top of them there loomed another vessel, so close that a man with a pistol might have sent a bullet into her bows across the narrow divide. There came a shout from the stranger's deck: a voice not Greek hailed them, crying, "Friend or foe?" and a babble of other voices followed. "It is a trap!", "Beware!", "The Greeks have sent a fireship to destroy us!", "Allah preserve us!"

Amid the hubbub there came the sound of pattering feet: it was the captain, making for the helmsman. "Lie quiet!" he hissed as he passed. "Let no man move! Let no man speak! Helm hard down! Down, I say!"

The order was obeyed: the fast little ship, darting like an arrow from the bow close under the frigate's looming stern, shot away into the darkness and was lost to Turkish sight as if she had been a ghost. It had all happened so quickly that there had been no time for the startled crew to betray themselves by an unwary shot: the very dogs had stayed quiet. Byron rendered silent thanks that their barking had not disclosed their whereabouts. It was, declared the captain, a miracle of all the saints! A sign from heaven that their enterprise was blessed: but Byron felt he would not breathe easily until daylight proved them safe.

The sun rose early on a calm and glittering sea and showed that his lordship's fears were well-founded. The little mystico was safe enough for the moment, in the coastal shallows where the Turkish brig could not follow: but that brig lay between them and Missolonghi. There was no question of reaching their destination directly: fast though the little ship was, the wind was against her, and the Turk was waiting her moment to pounce. Byron, looking through the glass, had other cause for concern. There was the bombard, some miles distant, but easily seen on this beautiful morning: and there was a second frigate bearing down upon her. And in the bombard was Pietro, with his papers and his money. He could only hope and pray.

Meanwhile, their own situation was parlous enough: they could not stay here forever, playing cat and mouse among the rocks. The frigate could not follow them herself, but she could always send her boats to intercept them, and their whole armoury consisted of two carbines and a fowling-piece. For himself he did not much care: but there was always clumsy, faithful Fletcher to consider, let alone the young Greek who had attached himself and refused to be dismissed.

Fletcher was surprisingly resigned. "This is a pretty kettle of fish, Mylord," he said. "I've been through shipwrecks with you, and earthquakes, and fever and I don't know what else, so what's being taken prisoner? Any man who's gone along with you all these years should be prepared for anything."

"Here's a change of front!" mocked Byron. "You can't be feeling well!" Fletcher frowned, and jerked his head towards the young

Greek: and Byron understood. For Loukas there would be no mercy shown if the worst came to the worst. For misguided foreign nationals there might be some clemency – there could be none for a Greek insurgent, however young. Byron felt a cold chill as he remembered some of the Turks' more engaging ways with their victims. There suddenly rose before his vision the memory of a dismembered body and a blackened, rotting head displayed for all to see: he caught Fletcher's eye and knew he shared the memory. But it would never do to scare the boy. He must turn it all to jest.

"I wonder," he said, voicing the first thought that came into his head, "if it's worth swimming for it?"

Loukas looked doubtful. "I do not think, Mylord, that I can swim so far," he said hesitatingly. "It is a long way to the shore."

"That's all right: you may climb on my back and ride like Arion on the dolphin."

"Well, I can't do it, Mylord!" declared Fletcher tartly. "We know that you're the next best thing to a fish but I can go only on dry land like a Christian, and well you know it!"

The captain had a better suggestion. "We should put a man ashore, Mylord, and send word to the English Colonel in Missolonghi. Could not the boy get through with such a message? I can spare a man to go with him."

"Yes, yes, Mylord! Only try me! I will do anything to help you! – Only try me! I promise I will not fail!"

Byron looked into the eager eyes and made up his mind. "Very well," he said. "We will tell them if we can what has happened and beg for an escort. It really is too bad of them: they might have told us that the Turks were at large again!"

So Byron hastily scribbled a note to Stanhope, dated, impishly enough, from "Scrofer (or some such name!) on board a Cephaloniote mystico, December 31st, 1823." It was light-hearted enough, but his anxiety for Loukas broke through and lent a note of urgency that should bring Stanhope hotfoot to the rescue.

"We are just arrived here," he wrote, "… but Gamba, and my horses, and the press, and all the Committee things, also some eight thousand dollars of mine … are taken by the Turkish frigates … Here we are, with the sun and clearing weather, within a pretty little port enough: but whether our Turkish

friends may not send in their boats and take us out ... is
another question, especially if we remain long here, since we
are blocked out of Missolonghi by the direct entrance. You had
better send my friend George Drake (Draco) and a body of
Souliotes to escort us by land or by the canals with all convenient speed. Gamba and our bombard are taken into Patras, I
suppose; and we must take a turn at the Turks to get them out:
but where the devil is the fleet gone? – The Greek, I mean:
leaving us to get in without the least intimation that the Mos-
lems were out again. Make my respects to Mavrocordato, and
say that I am here at his disposal. I am uneasy at being here:
not so much on my own account as on that of a Greek boy with
me, for you know what his fate would be: and I would sooner cut
him in pieces, and myself too, than have him taken by those
barbarians. We are all very well."

"There!" he said as he folded it. "Stow it in a safe place,
Loukas, and get it to Colonel Stanhope as fast as you can."

By now the mystico had drawn in as close to the shore as she
dared: Loukas and one of the sailors clambered over the side
and scrambled onto the rocks. "God go with you!" cried Byron.
"We will meet soon and laugh at all this!" He waved: Loukas
waved, turned, and disappeared from view. The captain said
urgently, "Mylord, Mylord, what now? I fear much that we are
lost – they have seen us!"

He was right – the frigate was heading steadily in their
direction, and there was no time to lose. Byron had no hesitation: he knew that his crippled leg would be a liability should
they land on the rocks and try to follow Loukas. "Push off!" he
directed. "Hug the coast in the shallow waters! We are so fast
we may yet give them the slip. We cannot stay here – their boats
could reach us in a trice: we must keep moving where they
cannot follow."

All that day they played hide-and-seek northward along the
rocky coast, flirting in and out of the rocks, with both sails
spread: but the enemy would not give up the chase and kept
always in sight like a sleeping cat waiting to pounce on this
infuriating mouse. Not until they reached a reasonable port
would Byron feel safe: but as night fell, harbour lights could be
seen to starboard, and they crept thankfully into the anchorage

of Dragomestri. At last they could breathe a sigh of relief, but it was only temporary. Mylord sent fresh messages for help, but as yet none was forthcoming: the nights were cold, and they still wore the clothes in which they had left Argostoli. Fletcher was once more sunk in gloom: he had a cold in his head and blamed Byron for it, since he had got so wet in Argostoli harbour. "That's not fair!" protested his lordship. "*I* wasn't rowing the damned thing."

"That's what I'm complaining about", sniffed Fletcher dolefully. "If your lordship had lowered yourself to do so we would all have stayed dry, and so – tishoo! – it *is* your fault."

"Are you blaming me or flattering me?" cried Byron – but he was secretly gratified all the same. He could not be downcast for long: like an overgrown schoolboy, he was revelling in the adventure. If only he could be sure of Pietro's safety he would have been as happy as a sandboy.

Pietro would have been even happier to be certain of safety. The morning light had shown him and everyone else on the bombard that journey's end was in sight, and in fact they must steer quickly clear of the rocks if they were not to come to grief. They were not alone: as Byron had seen from afar, another ship was slowly but steadily heading towards them, and Pietro thought, as everyone else did, that this was part of an escort sent to meet them. Of the mystico there was no sign: he could only assume that the faster ship had reached Missolonghi already. The ship drew closer: and so did the captain's brows.

"What's the matter?" demanded Pietro, suddenly on the alert.

"I am not happy, Count: I do not recognise this ship. Of one thing I am certain – she is no Spetsiot."

"How can you tell?"

"She is too large: she is not built in the Greek style. I wonder – Mother of God! Quick! Ring up our Ionian flag! Quick – quick! This is a Turk!"

There was a rush to obey him: the other vessel followed their example: and with growing horror those aboard the bombard saw her colours flutter to the masthead. In the green-gold light of a cold, crisp dawn the crescent threatened disaster: as it drew ever nearer a hoarse voice could be heard shouting.

"Your captain and your papers! Quick! Your captain must bring your papers! Or we fire!"

The crew were flapping about like hens with their heads cut off: Captain Valsamaki had turned pale under his tan. Pietro thought quickly: there was no time for elaborate plans.

"Do as he says," he said urgently. "Listen! We are an Ionian vessel – that is quite true, and our flag shows it. They dare not harm a neutral – I hope! Then tell him that we are in the service of an English lord – that is also true, and should frighten him a little. But we are going to the island of Kalamos. Have you got that?"

"But Count, that is far to the northward!"

"Never mind that! Just do as I say. Hurry! He's getting impatient."

The dinghy had by now been lowered and was bobbing about waiting for its passenger. Valsamaki, shaking in every limb, climbed gingerly down and rowed slowly over to the frigate. Pietro Gamba, fretting with impatience, stayed long enough to see him disappear over the enemy rail: then rushed off to save, if he could, the incriminating evidence.

"So!" he muttered to himself as he collected Byron's letters from Stanhope and Mavrocordato. "This – this – and this! What to use? Ah!" He wrapped the letters into as tight a bundle as he could, working swiftly, and tied a weight to the whole. Then he called his servant. "Come with me!" he ordered curtly, giving the packet into the man's hand. "Stand here behind the sail where no one can see you. So! It is well. Can you see everything that happens?"

The man nodded. He was pale but his hand was steady enough.

"Watch closely! And say nothing. Watch for a boat! If one comes to us, you are to drop that instantly – but instantly! – into the water. But do not let anyone see!" He frowned terribly – then smiled. "Do as I say, and all will yet be well!" he promised.

Time passed. The sun rose higher and higher, and the two ships remained motionless. The tension aboard the bombard was intense: Gamba's eyes were strained with watching nothing. His neck ached, and so did his head. He peered ahead even more intently and now he could see for himself a movement on board the frigate. A sailor appeared, climbed overboard and crept slowly, so slowly, down the rope ladder. There came a sound from behind him – a soft splash: and without turning his head he knew that Mylord's letters had gone into the Gulf. Pietro let his breath go in a long sigh. Let them come – they would find nothing. Then, as if sensing that his mission would be fruitless, the sailor climbed back again and disappeared over the rail of the frigate. Time passed. The sun rose higher in the sky, and Pietro's nerves were stretched to breaking point. Over on the horizon a small white cloud appeared. It came steadily nearer and divided into three. Pietro groaned aloud. This was no cloud, but the sails of reinforcements. So that was why the Turk had made no move. She had also seen those sails, now coming up fast: the hoarse voice called again across the narrow divide. "You are my prisoner! You must surrender! We go to Patras! Follow me, or I will sink you!" Bereft of their captain, terrified of what might befall, the panic-stricken crew hastened to obey: they dared not do otherwise. Pietro ground his teeth. For a wild moment he hoped that they might yet escape, but it was only for a moment. The bombard was far too slow, and the crew, whimpering and weeping as they hauled the sheets, would never defy their orders. Maddeningly, the shore of Missolonghi receded: he could only hope that Byron had succeeded in avoiding capture.

Suddenly, he heard a voice shouting his name, and turning, he saw that Spiro Valsamaki was waving to him from the frigate's quarterdeck. "It is all right!" he bellowed. "Be of good courage! Everything is arranged – by me! It is all right! We meet in Patras!" Pietro could make nothing of it, but bethought him that it would be as well to be prepared for a confrontation. Accordingly, he seized a telescope and a bottle of rum from below decks – he had a feeling they might come in useful.

He was right. The Turkish commander of the frigate had discovered in Spiro not only an old acquaintance but one who in more peaceful days had saved him from shipwreck. "I will do anything for Spiro!" he declared. "Anything in this world to which he preserved me. What are you doing, hey? Don't tell me – you go to Missolonghi to the Greek rebels – I know!" and he laughed uproariously.

With what dignity he could muster, Pietro disclaimed all knowledge of the partisans. "I serve an English nobleman," he declared, with truth. "We are going to join him at Kalamos." He hoped he made a good liar. Zacharia Bey roared with laughter again. "No, no, my friend, you are for Missolonghi!" he cried. "Spiro has told me – but all will be well for you. I owe him a little something, that one, and I will tell for him a little lie, and you will be let go. Thus does a Turk pay his debts." He stood up proudly. "Come, my friend!" he said. "We will arrange all – over dinner!"

***

It was Monday morning, and Missolonghi was en fête. The streets were a seething mass of people, old and young, sick and hearty, all making their way to the edge of the lagoon. Three miles across the polluted waters a long, low vessel had let down her anchor the previous night, and the word had spread like wildfire that Mylord Byron was safely come at last. Even now, Mylord was being rowed across those malarial swamps, and when the first keen-eyed watcher spotted its dark shape a tremendous cheer arose from every throat. It was eleven in the morning when a slight and halting figure stepped onto the shore, clad this time not in the frogged green jacket in which he had landed at Argostoli but in the brave scarlet regimentals lent to him by his friends of the 8th Regiment of Foot: and the crowd went wild. Waving and yelling they surged round him and practically carried him, flushed and happy, to the house where a lodging had been provided for him. The crashing of welcoming cannon, the beating of drums, the pop-pop of muskets and the enthusiastic cheers coming up from the harbour had been warning enough: his friends were all there at the door to meet him. His gaze swept eagerly over them. There was Mavrocordato, peering through his gold-rimmed spectacles: Stanhope, of the burning conviction: there was a little knot of officers, Greek and European, and – there, to his intense delight and relief was the fair, boyish face of Pietro. How he had escaped from his captors he could not guess, but there he was, and Byron held out both hands as Pietro ran to embrace him with tears of joy.

"Mio Bairon!" he cried, using Teresa's own term of endearment. "It is you! You have come! Thank God! Thank God! I have been so worried!"

"*You* have been worried!" teased Byron, shaking him gently by the elbows. "How have I felt? The last I saw of you, Johnny Turk all but had you in his clutches! Let us get inside, and you shall tell me all about it. Prince!" He turned, and held out a hand to Mavrocordato, who was almost bursting with emotion. "Stanhope! Gentlemen all, I thank you for your welcome, and I am most happy to be with you all at last."

Stanhope came forward, eager and important. "Mylord, you must come inside at once and refresh yourself! We will hold a consultation immediately, so that you can see for yourself how matters stand. I wish that we could have arranged more commodious quarters for you but alas! There are none better to be had."

"Oh, as to that, I'm sure we shall do very well," replied Byron as he followed Stanhope into the house. But he had to admit to himself that his quarters were spartan enough, and though the house was reasonably large it was bursting at the seams. It belonged to the Primate Capsali, and it was clear to Byron that Stanhope had been quick to seize the best of the accommodation for himself. "And why not?" thought his lordship charitably. "He was here first, after all!" There was a courtyard with several useful outbuildings which, together with the ground floor rooms, were filled with Greek soldiers. The middle storey, apart from the landlord's own rooms, was taken over by Stanhope: and the whole of the top floor was to be Byron's domain. "And so," he said, "I am the nearest to heaven, after all!" as he chose two front rooms overlooking the lagoon for his own use, leaving those looking on to the courtyard for Pietro and the rest of his entourage. The whole house was sparsely furnished, and the prevailing impression was one of damp and decay. Byron shrugged, and left the glowering Fletcher to make what he could of it. For himself, he must first find out what had happened to Pietro. He listened to his story with amazement mingled with amusement.

"So the Turk actually compounded your lie?" he asked incredulously.

"He did: which I certainly didn't expect from a man who would capture a neutral flag. However, the Pasha swallowed it – or at any rate he swallowed the fine woodcock I sent him: I had some very good shooting while I kicked my heels awaiting my fate. They have good sport in Patras! All the same, it was an unbelievable relief when he let me go – *with* all our possessions!"

"Have you got the money?" asked Byron quickly.

"The money and everything else but your letters," Pietro assured him. "We dropped those into the sea."

"Ah, that was well thought of!" said Byron, and Pietro glowed. "And we still have the money, which is the main thing – so all's well that ends well. I didn't really expect to see you here, you know!"

"Do I not! but I expected to see *you*, when I arrived yesterday."

"So would I have done, but for a most unlucky squall that blew us onto the rocks. Never mind that now – you shall hear all about it, later. Here comes our war cabinet! Now, Prince," he said to Mavrocordato who came into the room closely followed by Stanhope, "tell me how matters stand."

"At present, Mylord, we have a breathing space. The Sultan has withdrawn his army for the winter, but it is very certain that in the spring he will make a concerted attack on us here – we are the key to the Morea, and so to all Greece!"

Byron's mind was working quickly, "And the Pasha is in Patras, and commands the Gulf of Corinth. Had you any thoughts of an initiative of your own?"

Mavrocordato was puzzled. "I do not see –" he began.

"But I do! We should plan to take one of his strongholds, not wait for him to attack ours. How say you to – Lepanto?"

Mavrocordato's mind worked slowly, but he got the point.

"Lepanto? It is a thought!" he said. "You mean – we should attack Lepanto?"

"Yes," said his lordship patiently. "I do. Missolonghi would then be safe. So would your reputation."

Mavrocordato's enthusiasm caught fire there. "Aye! Indeed!" he cried. "Then our rich English loan will certainly come, and Greece will be free – liberated – rich! My friend, I kiss your hands!"

"First," said Byron dampingly, "you must attack Lepanto – and you must win! The Turkish army is strong, and brave, and well-disciplined. Is yours?"

The answer was unexpected – and it told all. A confused noise sounded outside: the door flew open, and in tramped several fierce-looking gentlemen all demanding, at the tops of their voices, that Mylord should consult with them at once. Each claimed precedence over all the others, Mavrocordato bleated helplessly at them, and Byron felt that he had strayed into a madhouse.

"For God's sake!" he cried. "One at a time!"

No one took any notice: to be fair, they were making so much noise that his soft voice had no hope of being heard. He clapped his hands angrily. There was an instant silence: and a remembered voice in his mind said, "Flaunting your lordly title again?" while another replied, "It comes in useful, you see!" The memory slid away: he said coldly, in the here and now, "Gentlemen, I am glad to see you: but I cannot possibly hear you if you all speak at once. Also, I am tired and hungry. I have had a long and difficult journey: I have not yet dined. If you will put your views in order, I will most gladly discuss them with you – separately – after the dinner hour. Until then, I must beg you to withdraw."

For a moment the issue hung in the balance: then one, taller and hairier than the rest, nodded agreement. "It is well!" he said. "We will wait upon your lordship this evening, and we will discuss with you the future of our glorious campaign. Death to the oppressor! Eleutheria!" He raised his hand aloft in a salute: a cheer that threatened to shake the roof right off the rafters reverberated round the shabby little room: and to Byron's intense relief the whole lot surged out again and clattered down the wooden staircase with much shouting and clamour. Byron sank his head into his hands. "Are they always like this?" he asked.

Stanhope smiled superciliously: Mavrocordato looked apologetic.

"I fear so, Mylord," he said. "They are excited, you see, and eager to chase the oppressor from our land."

"Then they must learn discipline," said Byron with asperity. "If their leaders are so wayward, how can they expect their men to be obedient?"

Mavrocordato blinked behind his spectacles. "It will be difficult, Mylord," he said. "You see, they are so very proud, and they are jealous of their position. They will accept orders from you, yes, but not from each other."

Byron sighed. "In that case," he said, "we must begin at the beginning: and all the men must drill every day. We have a natural parade-ground here in the courtyard, and the officers, too, must participate. And most of all – I will have no interruptions at all hours. I will see them here, every morning, and we will hold a proper conference: but they must not think that they can come charging in at will whenever they feel like it."

Mavrocordato blinked again. "It will be difficult," he repeated.

It was difficult, unbelievably difficult: but gradually the little army began to be knocked into shape. With the help of Stanhope and Mavrocordato, Byron began the recruitment of an artillery brigade, helped in this by all the flotsam of Europe that had drifted into the Morea once the war had begun. It was slow work, but gradually the corps took shape: and Byron decided that the brave but excitable Souliotes should form the core of another brigade, this time of infantry. And Byron was tired – tired by the constant noise, tired from having so much thrust upon his own narrow shoulders. Stanhope, impatient of Byron's caution, eager to be up and doing, was buzzing about like a trapped bumblebee, furious that Byron should seem so scornful of his propaganda efforts.

"You do not realise, Mylord," he said contemptuously, "the immense power and influence of the press." Byron, who had suffered more than most at the hand of hostile rumour, retorted that he knew more than most men. "What you forget," he said dampingly, "is that the strongest homilies in the world are useless if your audience is illiterate." It got Stanhope on the raw: his mouth went white, and he could hardly trust himself to speak.

"The liberty of the press," he said, in a trembling voice, "is essential if a state of anarchy is to be prevented!"

"Oh, undoubtedly," said Byron, with the utmost cordiality. "You are welcome to try: but it is arms which will finally win the day after all."

"I am a mere soldier," replied Stanhope, "and I am well aware – well aware, Mylord – that the army must fight the final battles. But I cannot deviate from my liberal principles. We had best, perhaps, avoid the subject in future." And for days he went about with a wounded expression.

Then there was Mavrocordato himself: eager and honest enough, but uncertain, vacillating and too anxious to please everyone. With the inevitable result, thought Byron, that he pleases no one! He lacked authority: blinking owl-like through his spectacles he would wait hopefully for a problem to go away. In Byron's experience, problems never did, and one of the most awkward was of Mavrocordato's own making. He had been surprised, himself, to be handed, one evening, a real live Turkish prisoner. To be honest, he hadn't the faintest idea what to do with the man, such things being the army's province, and he breathed a sigh of relief when Byron, hearing of this unexpected coup and not trusting the ruffians of his own brigade not to precipitate a crisis by indulging in vindictive behaviour, asked as a personal favour to allow him to take charge of the captive. The following evening, discussing the Lepanto project in his lordship's sitting-room, there came the sound of an altercation outside. Fletcher's voice could clearly be heard, shouting,

"No you don't! You get out of this!" There was a thud, a stamping of feet on the staircase, and the door was thrust rudely open. Mavrocordato, from his seat on the shabby divan looked up open-mouthed, blinking as usual as two be-whiskered Greeks burst in.

"Which one of you is Mylord?" sneered the bigger of the two. Mavrocordato shrank back: but an icy rage seized Byron. He started up, tight-lipped and pale.

"Get out!" he spat, with a viciousness that surprised himself.

"We will get out, my little lord, when we get back our prisoner," the man growled. "When we go, he goes with us – do you understand?"

"You will get out now, and alone!" said Byron between his teeth, and Mavrocordato saw with horror that the Greeks faced a suddenly-levelled pistol. "Out – or I shoot!"

The smaller man backed rapidly out of the room, his eyes never leaving those of his lordship: the other stood his ground for perhaps ten seconds longer. Byron slammed the door behind them and turned on his colleague.

"You pigeon-heart!" he said. "Have you no sense of discipline – of authority – of leadership? Had you shown the least bit of firmness from the start, this kind of insubordination could never have happened. By God, I begin to think the Turks are in the right of it!" He could hear a voice from the past say, "These animals need a soldier like myself to enforce discipline. Else all is in chaos." He wondered where Vasilly was now – if indeed he was still alive. He could not bear to fight Vasilly! Not even the humble apology proffered next day by the men's commanding officer served to placate him. They must beg pardon themselves, and the incident could then be considered closed, but "You will also," he said coldly, "apologise to my servant, whom you knocked down." He discovered that other prisoners were languishing in Greek hands, and sent them back to the Pasha with a letter of thanks for the return of Count Gamba. But he knew he could never feel real confidence in his ally again, much as he appreciated his innate honesty. The determination was lacking.

And there was always the weather. Even in fine weather, the marshland tended to creep uninvited into the streets: when it rained, those streets themselves became swamps, and the rain came down incessantly. Byron remembered Missolonghi as a tidy and active little town, but it was so no longer. The only drain lay down the middle of the main street and all kinds of rubbish went into it, thrown with careless abandon. Rotting vegetables, dead dogs, human and animal excrement went the same way and was diluted only by the green slime which crept in from the marshland and the salty ooze of the lagoon. The stench was indescribable: fish, garbage, sweat and slops mingled in an unsavoury pot-pourri: bedraggled and infested fowls chooked wanly in the sludge. The floppy white kilts of the Souliote soldiers were splashed with filth as they hop-scotched over the puddles. It was a mournful prospect. Byron thought with mortification that it was all his own fault: with any luck he would wake next morning from the nightmare to the scent of the orange trees and Teresa's long blonde hair rippling across the pillow.

It was brought in upon him in no uncertain manner that they had left the Lepanto project too late. News came of the worst kind: the Turkish fleet had made a sortie out of Patras and the Greeks, in a panic, had fled before them. The soldiers and citizens came to blows in the mud and sludge of Missolonghi: the townsfolk dimly felt that it was all the army's fault and that they would be left defenceless to the enemy, sure to come and wreak savage reprisals on them. They were soon calmed, but the rumour was all too true: Missolonghi was once again blockaded.

Byron refused to be dismayed. "If there is nothing to be done, there is no point in worrying," he declared philosophically, and surprised them all one morning by walking into the room waving a paper. "You were complaining the other day that I never write any poetry now. This is my birthday, and I have just finished something which, I think, is better than what I usually write. On this day, I complete my thirty-sixth year. So you will all sit quietly, if you please, and hear my verses! I may not be able to say so to you next year."

"I wonder," said Pietro Gamba, "if any of us will be here next year to celebrate the occasion? Much may happen in a year."

"Much indeed," said Byron with a crooked smile. "Well, others may do as they please – but I shall stay here – *that* is certain."

"If only," said Pietro, "our money and reinforcements would arrive, we could conclude this business the more speedily! The Committee promises this and that and still we wait. We were promised an artillery officer months ago – the men are becoming restless – we have missed our great opportunity – and still he doesn't come!"

"O ye of little faith!" mocked Byron. "Wait long enough and all things will come to pass!"

But neither of them had much longer to wait. A few days later footsteps were heard on the stairs and a burly figure trod over the threshold with Stanhope at his heels, picked out Byron in one swift glance and saluted. "Major William Parry, Mylord, at your service!" it said. "I believe you have been expecting me!"

***

Stanhope was looking aggrieved. It was bad enough, he thought, for Parry to arrive so late: but to ask for money the minute he arrived was the outside of enough. Besides, he hadn't got any, and if he had – he would have said exactly the same. "His Lordship is in charge of the war-chest: you had best apply to him."

"Ay, and so I shall!" Parry had answered, swiftly. "Where shall I find him, hey?" He was angry and ashamed that he should be obliged to beg from so exalted a personage, and before they had become acquainted, too. He need not have worried. Byron, seated on a cushion to soften the hardness of the divan, rose at once and held out his hand. "Welcome to Greece!" he said, with the sweet disarming smile that had caused so much havoc in the past. "We have indeed been expecting you these many weeks: now I have hopes that something may be done! Your arrival has taken a load off my mind." He looked quizzically at the newcomer, who looked anything but at ease himself. "You do not look pleased," he said. "Now, why? Perhaps you will feel better after you have refreshed yourself. Tita!" he cried, opening the door. "Tita! Bring some brandy and water, as quick as you can. Major Parry needs a restorative – and so, I think, do I!"

The brandy duly arrived. Parry didn't look any happier, but he found his tongue at last. "My situation, Mylord, is irksome inasmuch as I have come to help the Greeks as best I can but have no funds to do it! I have with me twelve men – eight English mechanics and four officers and I cannot pay them. Colonel Stanhope cannot assist me – he advised me to apply to you – and it is not the way I would have wished to introduce myself to your lordship's acquaintance."

Byron whirled on his heel. "Is that all?" he asked with relief. "I was afraid it was something else. Do not let that give you any uneasiness: you have only to tell me all your wants, for I like candour, and as far as I can, I will assist you."

Parry drew a long sigh of relief: but Byron heard Teresa's voice echoing in his head: "They only want your money." Well, perhaps he had been a fool to come: at the same time he knew that he could not have stayed away. And anyone could be forgiven for feeling depressed in this atrocious weather. If only the rain would stop! It was impossible to set foot outdoors: they had to go everywhere by rowing-boat across the foetid lagoon, and Pietro and Loukas had both succumbed to ague. Parry's precious stores had arrived, and had been left on the quay in the deluge. The day was a public holiday, it seemed, and nothing would be done about them until the morrow. Byron, at the end of his tether, lashed out at the startled Greeks. "You have had my purse: you have had my health!" he stormed at them. "My energies are devoted to your cause – but how *can* I help a people who will not help themselves? Tomorrow, you tell me – always tomorrow! And by tomorrow the powder and the armaments will be sodden, rusted and useless! Well, if you will do nothing about it, *I* will – I cannot and will not tolerate this senseless waste!" Throwing his heavy cloak over his shoulders, he went out into the deluge, down to the quay, where the packing cases were piled any old how. He lugged and tugged at them, dimly aware of voices calling to him, "Mylord! Mylord!" and blinking through the downpour he saw a knot of Greek soldiers, with Tita behind them, like a giant goosegirl shooing a flock of recalcitrant ganders. He paused, with the rain streaming down his face, until they came sheepishly up to him. "Well," he snarled, "what do *you* want?"

"Mylord, it is not fit for you to do this labourer's work!" said Tita. "You will do yourself an injury. Where do you want the stores put? Tell me, and I will see that these ingrates do it."

The ingrates murmured and looked sullen, but bent their backs to the task – they feared Tita's whiskers even more than the lash of Byron's tongue. Somehow the precious arms were got under cover, but his spirits were as dampened as his body. The English artificers brought by Parry were staggered by the filthy state of the town in general and their workplace in particular, and said so: he felt the whole weight of the war pressing ever more heavily upon him. He said bitterly, "it seems that I am to be Commander-in-Chief and the post is by no means a sinecure. Mavrocordato even addresses me as "archistrategos". And I came here as a civilian! As an adviser merely! But what do I find? – Nothing but muddle and corruption!" He sneezed violently: on top of everything, he had caught the inevitable cold.

Nevertheless, now that the essential artillery stores had arrived, he felt able to pursue again the Lepanto project, even though the renewed sea blockade would need to be breached if there were to be any hope of success, and he went on planning with dogged determination. But more than ever he knew that Vasilly had been right. So had Napier, who had warned him that he would need not only plenty of money but two English regiments and a portable gallows if he were to do anything with his mixed bag of Greeks. "Lion," he said to his dog one day, "thou art more faithful than men: thou art an honest fellow!" Lion barked and wagged his tail, delighted with the note of praise in his god's voice. Byron sighed. Strange, he mused, that to call a man "dog" should be an insult: the boot was so obviously on the other foot. Honesty certainly could not be laid to the Greek charge. Pietro, still pale and shaky, had set himself to unravel the tortuous accounts and found that the payroll contained names belonging to men no one had ever seen or heard of. The leak in Mylord's finances was plugged, but at a cost of much surliness and muttering from the army. The end came with ferocious suddenness, when the Souliote mercenary troops submitted an impossible demand. Half of them, they declared, were wasting their time and talents in the ranks: they should receive immediate promotion: they should be made generals, colonels, captains: and they should of course be paid accordingly. It was only their due for the dangerous and glorious exercise they were about to undertake in attacking Lepanto.

It was the end. "They only want your money!" mocked Teresa in Byron's memory: and he swore that this time they had gone too far. To their surprise, they found he really meant it: he dismissed them all summarily, declaring that the enterprise was at an end, that he had no confidence in persons to whom the words honour and duty were obviously meaningless, and that he washed his hands of the whole affair. He heard that voice in his head again: "Let them fight their silly war themselves!" and, by God, he would! "You are well named mercenaries," he said scornfully. "As greed means more to you than Greece, we will let Greece go. See if she will thank you!"

The delegation was startled: their leader opened his mouth to protest, but thought better of it. Pietro caught his eye and jerked his head silently towards the door: they shambled out, shamefaced and sullen. Next day the chief of them returned, begging an interview. Byron received him with cold dignity, listened to his protestations and finally agreed to take them back into his service: but it would be on his own terms. He would never trust them again, and the whole grandiose plan would be shelved. "You bear an honourable name, Constantine Botzaris!" he said. "Your kinsman did not count the cost in dollars, but with his life's blood. He passed the torch to you: and you have trampled it in the mire."

In self-defence, Botzaris said, "Mylord, I am too sensible of all the benefits you have conferred thus to abandon you. I have said that I will serve you as a common soldier if but five others will join me."

Byron snorted. "And will they?"

"Mylord, it is agreed that our army will disband so that no one who is unwilling shall be constrained. But all who are willing will submit to your discipline and accept your orders. Only – the assault must be abandoned. I cannot persuade them otherwise."

For a full minute the black eyes looked steadfastly into the grey ones: then Byron sighed, and said, "Very well. We will find some other means of ousting the Turk. But henceforth you will obey me implicitly: and you will not quarrel among yourselves any longer, for that I cannot – will not – tolerate! Is it understood?"

"It is understood, Mylord. Rest assured, we will live at peace one with another."

Byron held out his hand: the other shook it, and next minute his boots could be heard clumping down the staircase.

Mylord heard him go: then he sat slowly down and sank his head on his arms. He was crushed with disappointment. His great plan lay in fragments at his feet: his dreams of a great military coup had been shattered by the very people it aimed to liberate. He felt sick and humiliated. "It isn't even my own country!" he cried inwardly. "Yet I would have gone and fought for them who will not do it for themselves." He must lie down: he must lie on his bed and hope for oblivion.

Later, much later, a worried Count Gamba peeped into the darkened bedroom. "Come in, Pietro: I am not asleep. I am not well," said Byron.

"We wondered where you could be," said Pietro, sitting on the edge of the divan. "I thought perhaps you had gone out somewhere."

"There is nowhere for me to go," answered Byron dully. "It's all over, you know: the great enterprise. I have wasted the whole winter. What else has been wasted?"

The door opened again, and Parry tiptoed heavily in. His ruddy face was full of concern. Byron laughed weakly. "The waters of the flood are upon the earth," he said, "and they came in one by one unto Noah." He laughed again, at Parry's look of uncomprehending consternation. "Never mind," he said, "I shall be better presently."

Parry said, with concern, "You have the headache, Mylord. I will bring you a bracer: you will be restored in no time!" He left the room and returned in a very few minutes with a brimming glass.

"What is it?" asked Byron suspiciously.

"Brandy and punch, Mylord: my own recipe! I have never known it to fail."

Byron looked sceptical, but he took the concoction and drained it. "My God!" he said, choking. "It will be kill or cure, Parry, and the blame will be yours in either case! Leave me now – I shall try for some sleep. Don't look for me for at least three hours!"

It was rather more than three hours later when his halting step was heard coming downstairs, and Parry jumped up to greet him as he came into the room below. "How now, Mylord?" he cried, "How do you feel? Have you slept? Do you feel rested? Come and sit down!"

"Don't fuss me!" answered Byron. "I am well enough now – but I am so thirsty! I would like some cider, if there is any to be had."

"You shall have it immediately!" declared Parry, "but do, Mylord, temper it with a little brandy, You look flushed: I fear you have some fever!"

"No, no, I assure you I have frequently drunk cider alone and have never felt any untoward consequence."

Parry was forced to comply, and calling for Tita, gave him the order. Tita was back in no time: Byron seized the tankard from him and drank deeply. Parry watched him anxiously, as he set it down half empty.

"I needed that!" he said: then stood up, and said, in an uncertain voice, "Parry! I don't – feel –" He took a wavering step forward, staggered, and Parry leaped to his feet just in time to catch him as he fell. His body jerked convulsively: strong as he was, Parry could not hold him, and it took the combined efforts of himself and Tita to restrain his thrashing limbs. His mouth twisted to one side, and they could see his teeth tightly clenched as his lips writhed away from them. They managed to lay him down: the jerking of his body gradually eased: his eyes opened, and he said, in the thread of a voice, "Is it not Sunday?"

"Yes, Mylord," said Parry, subduing the tremor in his own voice, "it is Sunday."

"I should have thought it most strange if it were not," said Byron. "It has always been unlucky for me." Then, "The pain, Parry, the pain! Am I, do you think, like to die?"

Parry could only shake his head.

"Let me know," Byron went on. "Do not think I am afraid – I am not."

"I cannot tell that, Mylord – I am no doctor. Fletcher has gone for aid."

As he spoke, he became aware of a confused noise in the background. It had been going on for some time, but in his pre-occupation with Mylord it had not penetrated his consciousness. Now he heard it plainly: shouting and stamping mingled with the noise of running feet and the occasional discharge of a musket. The Souliotes were rioting again.

**

As riots go, it was short and sharp, but the confusion had done little to help the patient's recovery. At the first alarm the two Englishmen and Pietro Gamba had rushed out into the darkness, splashing their way to the arsenal. Byron, they felt with one accord, could safely be left to his medical attendants: their one thought was to save their precious ammunition from the mutineers. To nobody's great surprise they found that drink, not treason, lay at the root of the disturbance: nevertheless it was essential to make all safe and Byron, they knew, would be the first to agree. As it was, he was in no fit state to argue with anybody over anything: he lay drifting in and out of consciousness all night, while the anxious Dr Bruno kept nervous watch over his every movement. When morning came it found him weak and helpless, fearfully pale, but awake and aware of what was happening to him.

Bruno turned up the feeble lamp and peered anxiously at him. "How do you, Mylord?" he asked. "How do you feel?"

Byron looked dully at him.

I have no head, I believe," he muttered. "There is a heavy weight on my shoulders instead. It is pressing my brains out, I believe."

Bruno was dismayed, but tried not to show it. "In that case, Mylord, we must bleed you to relieve the pressure," he said.

At that, Byron started up in horror. "No!" he cried. "No and no and no! That I will never permit! I won't have it, you vampire! I'd sooner die! Fletcher, Fletcher, don't let him do it!"

"Now, Mylord, don't fret!" answered Fletcher, pushing him gently back onto the pillow. "If I can prevent it, no one shall bleed you. Dr Bruno will find another way."

"Mylord has always – always – had a horror of the lancet," said Fletcher. "Last time he was ill in these parts the physicians said he would die if he were not bled, but they did not bleed him and he did not die! Bring on your leeches if you must, but put the knife away."

Affronted, Bruno applied his leeches in silence to Byron's temples: but to everyone's horror including his own, he found it impossible to stop the flow when the creatures were removed. Terrified that his master would bleed to death, and blaming himself for pandering to his lordship's whims, Fletcher ran to the dispensary for Doctor Millingen. That stolid German, he felt, would at least keep his head in an emergency. Millingen came instantly, saw at a glance that the leeches had been placed too near an artery, and without hesitation applied caustic to the wound. Byron screamed, and fainted.

Into this scene of confusion walked Parry, straight from the disturbance at the arsenal, and stopped on the threshold transfixed with horror. Byron lay on his bed, ashen white, with blood trickling down his face and down the front of his nightshirt: Dr Bruno, himself in a state of semi-collapse, was wringing his hands helplessly at the bedside: Dr Millingen, horrified at the result of his efficacious but rough-and-ready methods, stood rooted to the spot: while Fletcher, utterly distraught, held his master in his arms with a face almost as white as his lordship's own.

"Foreigners!" snorted Parry. "Useless, every one of them! Here, you!" he called to Tita, who alone appeared to retain some sense of rationality (and that not much): "burn this under his lordship's nose! and tell me, where is the brandy?" As he spoke, he had been tearing the bands from his uniform jacket and slicing them into small pieces. "Burn them!" he repeated, "and mind you don't burn him into the bargain!"

He went in search of the brandy: when he returned he found Byron looking a shade less pale and he saw with relief that the blood had ceased to flow and was drying rapidly on his cheeks. Tipping the bottle onto his fingers he began to rub the spirit into his lordship's temples and across his lips, while Fletcher looked on with wonder, Tita with approval, Millingen with disdain and Dr Bruno with hope. It seemed a long moment before his lordship stirred: then he opened his eyes, looked at Parry in bewilderment and said in the echo of a voice, "You, Parry! Thank God it's you. Ah, the pain – there is nothing but pain!"

Pain or no pain, he struggled up on to his elbow and Bruno burst into tears of relief. Byron smiled his crooked smile. "Fear not, my friend," he said, "I'm not dead yet: at least, I do not think so. Do the dead feel so helpless?"

Before anyone could attempt to answer, there came a renewed hullabaloo from outside: there was confused shouting, a sound of trampling feet, and the next instant the door of the stuffy little room burst open and in rushed a band of dirty, wild-eyed Souliotes, waving their weapons above their heads and bawling incomprehensibly. In vain Parry and Tita tried to push them out: not even the gigantic Italian could do anything against their drunken strength, when to everyone's amazement a cool, calm voice cut like a sword through the hubbub.

"How dare you – how dare you," cried Byron, "come unasked into my bedchamber? If you have any grievances you may put them to your officers and I will talk to them – when it pleases me. It passes all bounds – I will not endure it. Out!"

For an instant the outcome hung in the balance. Whether it was his ghastly aspect, for he looked like a man newly risen from the grave, or the note of authority to which they were unaccustomed, no one could tell, but slowly the Souliotes lowered their weapons, looked with surly respect at the bloodied figure before them, and shambled slowly out of the room and down the stairs. Parry locked the door after them: he turned to find Byron sitting on the bed with a strange gleam in his eyes. He was laughing. "Away with your medicines!" he said gaily. "It seems all I need to cure me is anger! I have had enough of these fellows: I will get well, and see to them."

Byron spoke with too much optimism when he spoke of a cure: he was still pale next day and his legs showed a shameful tendency to wobble at the knees, but he had recovered his spirits and his enthusiasm. He was going through his accounts (never an easy task, for Lega had a strange method of book-keeping which no one could understand, including himself) when news came of a fresh excitement. Pietro came running upstairs, all in a glow about it. "Bairon!" he cried, "Bairon! We have a prize! There is a Turkish brig o'war run aground! I shall be avenged!"

Byron started up, sending his papers flying. "Why, that is capital!" he cried. "That will teach them to come skulking where they are not wanted! What is being done – if anything?"

"Here comes Parry. He is in charge – he will tell you!"

Parry came hastily in, burly and beaming. "You've heard the news, Mylord? The brig will certainly be ours – we will bring our guns to bear in a trice and she cannot possibly get away before we take her. Useless to wait for the tide! We have her at our mercy. See here!" He grabbed one of the unlucky papers, heavily crossed out, and, turning it over, began to rapidly sketch the brig's position. "Here is the shoreline – she has gone aground *here*. We will bring the cannon up here – and here – ready to fire at the slightest attempt at salvage."

"Is she alone?" asked Byron.

"By no means – there are others in the offing but they cannot come to her assistance without coming themselves within range."

"Excellent! Even so small a success will act, I hope, as a fillip to our fellows. How soon do we set out?"

"*We*, Mylord?"

"Yes, *we*."

Parry said, "No, Mylord. You must not make the attempt."

Byron felt his blood running hot. "Of course I shall come!" he said. "It is important even on so small a mission that I should be seen. It's a poor sort of commander who stays at home. I won't do it."

Pietro said, "Bairon, it is out of the question. You have been very ill – you are weak – your eyes are inflamed. Indeed, you must not venture."

Byron would have argued the point, but Parry cut in swiftly, saying in his blunt way, "Gamba is right. A sick commander is a liability. You must nurse your strength for the real fight."

"If it ever comes!" said Byron, depressed. Then, "Of course you are right. Tell them that I will give a reward for every Turk captured alive. If that doesn't inspire them to great deeds I know not what will."

He would no doubt have been proved right if the Turks hadn't stolen a march on them. How it happened no one quite knew: but her crew not only managed to escape with their stores to Patras, but before Parry's guns could open fire there came a dull boom from somewhere in her bowels and she exploded in a blossoming shower of sparks. It was unbelievable, but it had happened. For the first time Byron's hitherto unbounded confidence in Parry was shaken. "It is all the fault of those lazy Greeks!" he stormed. "If they had not left the powder to ruin in the rain it would not have happened so!"

"Perhaps," said Stanhope, coolly, "it is all the fault of Mr Parry! If he had known his business, the brig would be ours this minute. Wet powder or no, he should have hit a captive target." He was not altogether displeased. He pressed home his advantage. "You see now, Mylord, how essential it is to inspire the Greeks with patriotic fervour, to induce them to act together if they are to achieve success. You laugh at my printing-press, but admit that it has united Greece in a way that our friend Parry has yet to do."

"Oh," burst out Byron, "you suffer from liberal indigestion! You have taken an overdose of Bentham on an empty stomach! What is admirable in theory is not always so in practice, and it will not do! High ideals are all very well, but in the end the battle must be won by the sword. The enemy does not read your propaganda!"

Stanhope controlled himself with an effort. He clenched his fist until the knuckles were white: his mouth was almost invisible. He said, "The enemy is not impressed with incompetent artillery either, it would seem."

Byron's shoulders sagged. "No," he said. "No. The answer stares us in the face, and it lies in one word – discipline. That is all the Turk's secret, and we have none."

In fact, there was even less than he knew. All that day and far into the night, Pietro had sat on the beach and watched the brig's funeral pyre: and when he returned in the morning he found the house in a complete state of chaos and uproar. "What has happened?" he cried, seizing Stanhope by the arm. "What's the matter?"

"What's the matter? Murder's the matter!" snapped Stanhope.

"Who – not his lordship?"

"No, no, he's safe. It's those damned Souliotes again, and this time they've gone too far!"

Pietro could get no more out of him but little by little he pieced together what had happened. It seemed that while he had been on the beach, watching the last flaming spars sink into the waters, one of the Souliotes, a man named Toti, had offered, as a treat, to show his chief's little nephew the guns stored in the arsenal. At least, that was his story: the more sceptical saw it as an ingenious effort to break in, and certainly the sentry on guard thought so.

"Halt!" he barked. "Who goes there?"

"I," answered Toti, with insolence. "Open for me and the little chieftain."

"I open to no one," retorted the guard. "Show me your permit!"

All he got for answer was a hefty shove. He let out a yell of alarm and the sergeant of the guard, seeing the fracas, ran up and grabbed Toti by the arm. It was too much for his fierce temper, and he aimed a punch at the sergeant that knocked him flat. By now others had come running up, and the Swedish officer of the guard, seeing his subordinate in difficulty, drew his sword and struck Toti a blow with the flat of the blade. By now in a blind rage, dimly hearing the child's frightened sobs, and jealous of his honour, Toti lost his head completely. He drew both pistol and dagger. There came a groan, and a thud. It was all over in an instant: but when it was over, Toti stood, sullen and appalled, his arms pulled tightly behind his back by two of the guard: the child cowered in a corner with his hands hiding his face: and Lieutenant Sass lay in the rain, staring with sightless eyes at the weeping heavens. There was a neat round hole in his head, and his left arm lay a little way from his body, the fingers curling up as if in supplication.

It was the sight of that severed arm that cooled the iron in Byron's soul. The world spun back: he saw, not the slim white hand of the Swede, but a hairy relic dangling from a tree: the start of his Grecian commitment and – perhaps – the end. "It is enough!" he said under his breath. "I can do no more with them – they must go."

A fresh clamour broke out in the courtyard: the Souliotes were yelling for their comrade's release, threatening to burn down his prison if he were not set free. "And he with it, I presume," said Byron ironically. "My mind is made up – they must go. Or they can stay and I will go. In truth, I care not which! I cannot and will not tolerate broken promises any longer." Two remembered voices beat in his brain, one feminine, sweet and musical, saying, "They only want your money"; the other, deep and cynical: "So much for the morality of the modern Greek!" They were both right, thought Byron drearily: I denied them, and I was wrong.

He was still in his mood of disillusion as he stood in the rain next day by Sass's newly dug grave and dropped the first heavy clod on the coffin: and he returned from the funeral to find that most of Parry's English artificers had announced their intention of returning home. "Let them go," he said wearily. "He that hath no stomach to this fight, let him depart: We shall do the better without them."

It said much for his recovery from that unexpected fit that he immersed himself next day in new plans for an offensive. Lepanto was now out of the question: but there was no reason why a less grandiose scheme should not be put into operation, and to this end he would rebuild his artillery brigade, recruiting from local patriots in place of the unruly Souliotes whose only regard for him was as a source of money. That be hanged for a joke! His old enthusiasm rekindled: he sent Stanhope off on a reconnaissance of the Morea and, "if you can get as far as Athens," he said, "I should be glad to have news of Trelawny. See if you can find how things look from there!" He would give Parry another chance.

"I know you are partial to brandy," he said with a smile, as they sat together after Stanhope's departure. "Let me have your opinion of this – and when you have done that, let me have your opinion as to the future of our little corps."

"As I see it, Mylord," Parry was beginning, when the contents of his glass suddenly slopped all over his breeches. The room swung violently about them: his chair overturned and both he and Byron were flung along the floor to end in a heap at one end of the room. Parry turned white: he yelled out in pure fright and cowered against the wall, cradling his head in his hands. The room steadied again: Byron looked at the shattered crockery littering the floor and pulled himself up. "It's only an earthquake," he said, wiping his fingers on his handkerchief. "But what a waste of good brandy."

"*Only* an earthquake!" cried Parry, fear giving a shrill edge to his voice. "I thought it was the end of the world."

"Oh no," said Byron. "I have known earthquakes before: but I will admit that this is the sharpest I can remember. Just listen to those silly fellows!" As a noise of shouting and the discharge of muskets sounded from below. "Placating the gods, no doubt!" He began to laugh. "A fit on Sunday," he chanted, "mutiny Monday, shipwreck on Tuesday, explosion on Wednesday, murder on Thursday, funeral on Friday, earthquake on Saturday – what comes on Sunday? Quite likely the end of Solomon Grundy!" and he ended with a peal of laughter.

It had been quite a week.

**

After the earthquake an uneasy peace settled upon the land and life returned to normal. Even the rain stopped falling, but under the surface disaffections still rumbled and threatened to boil over. Byron did not feel well: the strains of that momentous week had lowered his resistance and his vigour alike. At least the worst of the unrest was over, and the chiefs came dutifully to Byron and actually listened to what he had to say to them. What they said to the soldiers he did not know, but, subdued either by the murder or by their leaders' strictures. The barracks simmered down and there were no more disturbances. With relief, he turned to the immediate military problems.

The Lepanto project was dead and buried: he would think no more of it. But the brigade should be fully prepared against the day when other action called: and the fortifications of the town, after the heavy rains, were in urgent need of attention. In fact, his chief preoccupation now had to be political rather than martial: after all his high-minded talk about divided houses, thought Byron bitterly, it was perfidious of Stanhope to seek to cause a split between him and Mavrocordato. Especially now, when the Government was proving so co-operative. But so it was – Stanhope and Trelawny had become heavily embroiled with the army of Eastern Greece, and between them had hatched a plan to promote the war, with Byron's help, under the generalship of their new hero, one Odysseus Androutzos.

"All very well," muttered Bryon. "No doubt this Odysseus is all they say as a warrior, maybe more: but I remember him in the service of Ali Pasha, and a turncoat I never could stomach! What it really means is that here is another beggar with his hand held out for my purse." (They only want your money: they only want your money!) The words rang in his head, day after day.

Aloud, he said to Mavrocordato, "Well, Prince, what do you think of this proposal? My friend Trelawny writes to propose a Military Congress at Salona of ourselves and representatives of all the provinces. Do we go?"

Mavrocordato blinked nervously. "Mylord, I do not like it."

"No? Why?"

"I do not trust this Odysseus. And I do not trust the Colonel! He has never liked me – he wishes to remove me from any influence and to have things all his own way."

"Of course he does! It's as plain as the nose on your face – or on Trelawny's face, as his is a fine eagle's beak. Well! We will meet guile with guile and we will go and listen: but not just yet awhile. There are enough intrigues here to keep me fully occupied at present."

That was something of an understatement. Hardly a day passed without news of some plot: it seemed that every rogue and ruffian of the province had descended on Missolonghi to make trouble. He could not leave Missolonghi yet: somebody had to contain the continual outbreaks of tribal warfare – and his appeared to be the only authority anyone would recognise.

The climax came on the day when the town found that not only had a disaffected force occupied the landward forts but that the Turkish fleet had appeared at the entrance to the lagoon. The coincidence was too great: and Byron's own landlord's father-in-law, arrested on a charge of high treason, confessed with tears that yes, there had been a plan for joint occupation with the Turks to seize the town and Byron's dollars with it. ("They only want your money!") "Now there will be a massacre," he declared, "and I – shall die too, God help me!"

"There will be no massacre, if I can prevent it!" said Byron, very white about the mouth. "I have sworn to protect the people of Missolonghi and I will do so despite the traitors and cowards who are supposed to defend them! Summon my bodyguard! Summon my staff! We will ride out and reassure the people!"

It was an odd cavalcade that rode out among the people, dodging the puddles as it went. First came Byron's personal bodyguard: then the members of his household, so grandly called the "staff", in a strange mixture of brightly coloured uniforms: then Mylord himself, pale and gaunt but strangely impressive with his frogged green jacket and his gold-mounted pistols. It was pure bravado, but it worked. How the crowd cheered! They cheered little Loukas in his brave scarlet livery: they cheered big Tita, scowling and ferocious, looking bigger than ever in his silver-laced coat: but most of all they cheered Mylord, riding out so courageously to save them from the Turk.

For an hour or so the issue hung in the balance: but the rest of the army, swayed by none knew what impulse, came out against the traitors. The Turks withdrew: Missolonghi was saved.

Byron sank exhausted onto his divan. It was raining again: the roads were once more impassable. But even if they had not been, he knew he could not leave yet for any Congress. Stanhope could intrigue as much as he liked. Missolonghi had need of him and he must stay and be seen to have stayed. He could not do otherwise.

So he did stay: and he rode out whenever the weather permitted: and as long as he rode out the people who waved to him along the way felt secure from siege and betrayal, seeing in him a god sent to save them from the enemy within as well as from the Turk. One man in particular came to look for him every day, and Byron, spying the sturdy figure in the leather jerkin who saluted him so respectfully, came to look out for him as a talisman. "God save you, Mylord!" the man would shout lustily – but under his breath he whispered, "and only God can, I fear, for there is death in your face and then – God save us all!"

Ever since his first arrival in Missolonghi, Byron had left his horse at the town walls and was ferried back to his house across the lagoon. It had started as an accident and ended as a convention. "I have my own personal Charon!" he would joke, "who looks for my coming and will not be denied!"

"Deny him today," advised Gamba one afternoon when they had been caught in a violent rainstorm. "You are wet through already, you are perspiring: you will be chilled to the bone if you sit in a boat in all this rain!"

"You may ride home if you like," said Byron. "I am not so poor a creature, I assure you. I should make a pretty soldier indeed if I were to care for such a thing!"

Nettled, Gamba retorted, "What you dare, I dare! It is only water after all – and pretty stinking water too," he added, as they clambered aboard.

He did not later say, "I told you so," but he came very near it. He was wrestling as usual with the accounts when he heard a groan from Byron's room. Flinging down his pen, he went to see what was the matter. Byron was lying on his bed, shaking from head to foot. He looked up as Pietro came in and held out his hand. "You were in the right of it," he said. "The marsh fever has me again – this place will be the death of me! I do not care for death, but these agonies I cannot bear!"

Pietro said, "I will fetch Fletcher to you. He will know what to do: it is not the first time!" and went out of the room, hurriedly. Whatever Fletcher gave him seemed to help: he was almost himself again next day and insisted on riding out as usual. But in the evening the shudders had him once more in their grip, and his aching head and limbs were so painful that he grudgingly agreed that Dr Bruno should be summoned. "But I don't want to be physicked!" he grumbled. "I can't afford to be physicked! I have too much to do!"

Fletcher scolded him with rough affection. "You are your own worst enemy, Mylord," he told him. "You *would* ride out today on a damp saddle, and you see what comes of it. You will do exactly as Dr Bruno says."

Byron sank peevishly back upon his pillow. Dr Bruno came, tutted and said, "We must sweat the fever out of you, Mylord, and when we have done that we will send you to Zante for a little rest away from this pestilence-stricken place."

"I will not desert my post: I will not desert Missolonghi!" His eyes were very bright, his face flushed: Bruno said soothingly, "No, Mylord, you will not desert: you will go on sick leave merely. Now you must take a hot bath immediately, and then take a little castor oil, and you will see how much better you will feel tomorrow!"

But on the morrow the fever was still raging and Dr Bruno turned his thoughts once more to bleeding the patient. Byron turned his head impatiently. "No and no and no!" he said fretfully. "How many times must I tell you I will not be bled? No leeches, either! Look what happened last time I let you!"

"Mylord, your pulse is tumultuous! I will wait until tomorrow, but if you will not be bled you must at least take the medicine I shall prescribe!"

"Oh, very well," said Byron weakly. "I will swallow anything you like, but do not bleed me!"

He dutifully took the powders mixed by the careful Fletcher and seemed a shade better: he fell into an uneasy doze, but when the doctor saw beads of moisture break out on his brow he owned he felt hopeful that the fever was subsiding. Parry, coming to enquire how he did, was not nearly so sanguine. Indeed, he was shocked and alarmed by what he saw, and urged an immediate removal to Zante, away from the insalubrious air of Missolonghi. "You have lived in this sewer too long, Mylord!" he declared robustly. "Sweet island air will soon clear your head and your lungs together. You do quite right not to be bled – quite right. Brandy, Mylord, brandy is what you need: it is the only thing that will save you. Leave it all to me – I will see to everything!" And he bustled off, full of importance, leaving the twittering Bruno indignant.

"Brandy, indeed!" he said scathingly. "Enough to kill you outright, Mylord, with the degree of fever you have in you! You will take another hot bath, and another powder, and tomorrow – well, we shall see!"

Whether it was the bath or the powder or both together nobody knew, but Byron was so much restored that he got up, demanded a bowl of broth and declared himself ready to attend to business. It was too good to last, and on the following day Pietro found him sitting on the edge of the divan with his head sunk in his hands. He raised it as his friend entered, and said blearily, "It's no use, Pietro. There's a sledgehammer at work in my skull." Pietro laid his own cool hand on Byron's burning forehead, horrified at the heat he felt. He said calmly, "I will fetch Dr Bruno. Lie down and be quiet now!" And hastened off. In the passage he met Fletcher on his way to attend his master. He stopped him and said, "Fletcher, his lordship is very ill: it is worse than I thought! I believe he is in real danger."

Fletcher looked him in the eye: he said stolidly, "Yes, Count: I have thought so these last two days, but the doctor made light of it and I believed he must know better than I."

"Well, he does not! We must get his lordship away from this – this pit of putrescence – as soon as may be."

"You are too late," answered Fletcher. "Listen! Listen to the wind! You will hardly expect him to sail away in this!"

For the first time Pietro became aware that the wind had risen and that the rain was lashing down again. Hour by hour the storm grew worse, until it seemed that the howling wind would lift the roof right off the house. Water streamed down the windowpanes so that it was impossible to see out. There could be no putting to sea for days. In the stuffy little bedroom Byron tossed and turned: Dr Bruno and Dr Millingen held a hasty consultation at his bedside and turned their thoughts once more to bleeding to relieve the fever. "I tell you, NO!" said Byron, weakly. "The lancet kills more than the lance – I will not have it." His tongue was furred and filthy: Fletcher brewed some blackcurrant tea to relieve his thirst but the only effect was to make him vomit copiously. He lay back, holding his diaphragm and gasping. "Oh, go away, all of you!" he moaned. "Leave me alone, and let me sleep!"

So, reluctantly, the patient was left with only the faithful Fletcher to keep watch over him, ready to summon aid at a moment's notice. Byron lay silent for a while: then said, "Doctors! What do they know of anything?"

"What indeed, Mylord."

"They tell me that it is only a common cold which you know I have had a thousand times."

"I am sure, Mylord, that you never had one of so serious a nature."

"I think I never had." There was a pause, then he said, "We'll go no more a-roving, Fletcher. We have done much together, you and I. But now we'll go no more a-roving."

"Now, Mylord, these gloomy thoughts will never do! We'll have many an adventure together yet. Try for some sleep now."

"No, no, we'll go no more a-roving and it's late into the night. If I were not so thirsty!"

"I will fetch your lordship some lemonade. Do you think you could drink it?"

"Yes, yes, bring it! I will do what I can."

This time, it stayed down, and surprisingly, he slept the greater part of the night. Hopes revived next morning, when he declared himself to feel much stronger, though the fever flush still burned in his cheeks. Dr Millingen felt he was well enough to receive a talking-to. "Mylord," he said solemnly, "we have tried every other remedy out of consideration for your feelings: it is time now that you considered ours! Think of our reputations if you should miscarry!"

"I know what you are after," answered Byron. "NO!"

"Very well, Mylord: it shall be as you say: but I am sorry to see you show so little resolution."

Stung, his patient asked, "Do you call me coward?"

"Why, yes, Mylord, I do! You fear the knife: but you should fear the fever more, lest it attack the brain."

That did it. Angrily thrusting out his arm, Byron said, "There, you damned set of butchers! Take what you like, and have done with it!"

So at last they had their way: and, the operation completed, Byron sank back exhausted. He said, "When I am better, I will go."

"Certainly, Mylord. You will go to Zante – it is all arranged."

"No, no, I will go home. I will go home to Newstead – to my wife – to my child. I will beg her forgiveness, and she will forgive me – she is too noble not to! No man on earth respects a virtuous woman more than I do, and the prospect of retirement in England with my wife – and Ada – gives me an idea of happiness I have never experienced before. I will go – I am going home!"

Millingen's brows drew together. "It is delirium," said Bruno, in an undervoice. "No," answered the other. "It is death!"

By now the news of Mylord's illness had spread through the barracks and out into the streets. The townspeople were stunned. It could not be; it must not be! Heedless of the downpour, they made their way with one accord to the place where Byron lay, and gathered with hushed voices outside the house, waiting for they knew not what. In the forefront stood a man in a leather jerkin: his throat was working and his voice was harsh with unshed tears. "Said I not so?" he muttered. "I saw death in his face! There is no hope!"

Within the house, all that could be done for Byron's comfort was being done, with no effort being spared to reduce that soaring fever and to ease the pain in his limbs. He had slept fitfully all that day and night, waking to swallow the water held to his lips to assuage that raging thirst: from time to time he would mutter incoherently, but the disjointed words made little sense to the watchers round the bed. At times he gasped for breath and Fletcher, raising him in his arms to ease the breath-

ing, exclaimed in an agony, "Oh, to see such suffering! Would I
could bear it for him!"

"I do not think," said Millingen gently, "that Mylord is suffering now – I believe he has passed beyond pain."

Millingen was right. Mylord, floating beyond the dark, dank
little room, was dimly aware that somewhere far below there
lay a wasted being surrounded by well-meaning busybodies,
and felt a faint sense of pity for him. "Why don't they leave him
alone?" he thought. "Why don't they leave him in peace?" It was
nothing to do with him, for he was walking through the gaunt
corridors of Newstead towards a brilliant light that beckoned
through the arch at the far end. He saw with no particular
surprise the pale, drowned face of Shelley, walking beside him.
Ahead of them scampered a small figure in a white muslin
dress. "Papa, Papa!" she called in her childish treble, "Come and
catch me, Papa!" and skipped along in front of him, just out of
reach. They drew nearer to the end of the long passage and the
light, flooding through the archway, dazzled his eyes. For a
timeless instant he hovered on the threshold, blinded by that
white radiance. Then, with his friend holding one hand and his
daughter tugging at the other, he limped into the light.

As the light of late afternoon filtered through the shutters
Mylord opened wide his eyes: then closed them sharply as if the
dimming light of day were too strong for them to bear. Swiftly,
one of the physicians stepped to the bedside, and gently laid his
fingers across the quiet pulse.

Even as the watchers in that silent room heard the clock
chime the quarter hour, a flash of lightning splintered across
the sky and thunder cracked overhead. In the street, the man
in the leather jerkin seized his neighbour by the elbow and cried
aloud in anguish, "It is a signal from heaven! He is gone! The
great man is gone!"

Superstitious fears were awakened. The grief-stricken cry
was tossed back and forth through the town, carried on the
dying echoes of the thunder – "Byron is gone ... is gone ... is
gone!"

***

Provisional Government of Western Greece.

"The present day of festivity and rejoicing has become one of sorrow and of mourning. The Lord Noel Byron departed this life at six o'clock in the afternoon, after an illness of ten days; his death being caused by an inflammatory fever. Such was the effect of his Lordship's illness on the public mind, that all classes had forgotten their usual recreations of Easter, even before the afflicting event was apprehended.

"The loss of this illustrious individual is undoubtedly to be deplored by all Greece; but it must be more especially a subject of lamentation at Missolonghi, where his generosity had been so conspicuously displayed, and of which he had even become a citizen, with the further determination of participating in all the dangers of war.

"Everybody is acquainted with the beneficent acts of his Lordship, and none can cease to hail his name as that of a real benefactor.

"Until, therefore, the final determination of the National Government be known, and by virtue of the powers with which it has been pleased to invest me, I hereby decree –

"1st. Tomorrow morning, at daylight, thirty-seven minute guns will be fired from the Grand Battery, being the number which corresponds with the age of the illustrious deceased.

"2nd. All the public offices, even the tribunals, are to remain closed for three successive days.

"3rd. All the shops, except those in which provisions or medicines are sold, will also be shut; and it is strictly enjoined that every species of public amusement, and other demonstrations of festivity at Easter, shall be suspended.

"4th. A general mourning will be observed for twenty-one days.

"5th. Prayers and a funeral service are to be offered up in all the churches.

(Signed) A. MAVROCORDATO,

GEORGE PRAIDIS, Secretary

Given at Missolonghi,
this 19th day of April, 1824

***

CODA

By May of the year 1824, Europe had been at peace for nine years. Napoleon Bonaparte had died in solitary exile on the distant island of St Helena, dethroned, embittered and outcast. Europe, settling into the long placid years, would not see such another convulsion for a century. In Greece, the struggle was just beginning, as she roused from lethargy and sought to throw off the Turkish yoke.

One morning in this May of 1824, to the solemn boom of gunfire, a brig set sail from Missolonghi, with its curious double foreshore. It carried a doleful burden. Byron was going home, as he had said: home to the land he had left as a voluntary exile, scorned and reviled: home to his ancestors in the family vault, near the seat that was part of himself. Slowly the mountains receded beyond the mists and the marshes: and Missolonghi faded from view of the living as they turned their faces to the west, to the outer isles, the Mediterranean and England. Byron had, finally, turned his back on Greece.

The last voyage was smooth and stately: the last drive slow and sombre. This would be the second funeral service accorded to Mylord. A simple, moving farewell had been held by his followers in the crowded church of Missolonghi, and Mylord held court in state, while the people came to bid him goodbye with gratitude and grief. He lay in his simple, open coffin, watched over by the men of his personal bodyguard: crowned with laurel and with his sword at his side. Mavrocordato, blinking behind his spectacles, was blinking back the tears: Pietro Gamba was unashamedly weeping. "He died," he was reflecting, "in a strange land, and amongst strangers, but more loved, more sincerely wept he never could have been wherever he breathed his last. And I – I am left to tell Teresa – and so, to break her heart."

Now he had safely returned to his native land, escorted by Colonel Stanhope who, all differences forgotten, remembered only the efforts they had made together in a common cause – the cause, as he put it to the London Committee, of an oppressed nation, a cause to which "he sacrificed his comfort, fortune, health and life."

And so his cortege entered the last phase of the long, sad journey. As the procession passed slowly through the Hertfordshire lanes, a carriage paused to give it precedence: then turned and went back the way it had come, deflected by the mournful panoply of black velvet, black horses, black plumes. The carriage's occupant, small, blonde and delicate, never knew until the following day whose worn-out shell rested beneath the pall: nor did she ever know that round his neck as he died he wore a chain of golden hair – hair that was not her own. The silken leash had held him to the end.

SOURCES AND BIBLIOGRAPHY

BYRON — Poetical Works

HOBHOUSE, John Cam — A Journey Through Albania

MAUROIS, Andre — Byron

MAYNE, Ethel Colburn — The Life and Letters of Lady Byron

MOORE, Thomas — Life, Letters and Journals of Lord Byron

NICHOLSON, Harold — Byron – The Last Journey

ORIGO, Iris — The Last Attachment

QUENNELL, Peter — Byron in Italy

WHEELER, Private (Edited by Captain Liddell Hart) — Letters, 1809-1828

www.ingramcontent.com/pod-product-compliance
Lightning Source LLC
Chambersburg PA
CBHW051142020726
47501CB00005B/1638